MₗCₗ Se X

Hanging Party

Claiming to be wrongly accused of murder, drifter Rafe Lonis takes Diana Logan hostage and leaves Matt Sutton in his clothes to face a blood-mad hanging party. Now Matt must elude the posse if he's to save Diana.

Having caught up with them he, Diana and Lonis, now a prisoner, must fight their way through Indian country with the knowledge that one of the possemen is the mysterious murderer.

An iron-willed rancher and his gun-happy son add to the conflict before the murderer can be unmasked and brought to justice.

To the memory of
Marie Ardell White
Writer, Actress, Dancer
and
Loving Wife

Hanging Party

JAMES GORDON WHITE

A Black Horse Western

ROBERT HALE · LONDON

ISBN-10: 0-7090-8012-3
ISBN-13: 978-0-7090-8012-1

Robert Hale Limited
Clerkenwell House
Clerkenwell Green
London EC1R 0HT

Typeset by
Derek Doyle & Associates, Shaw Heath.
Printed and bound in Great Britain by
Antony Rowe Limited, Wiltshire.

CHAPTER ONE

When Matt Sutton and Diana Logan broke camp the morning held the promise of a fine, cheery spring day, but, as the day wore on, things gradually began to look less and less cheery. They tried to pay no nevermind and concentrate on reaching the distant woods and hills; being stuck out on the prairie in a storm wasn't healthy for man or beast.

The two had been on the trail to California for some time now, setting a leisurely pace and seeing the country, as it was doubtful they would ever pass that way again. Naturally, there had been a few unforeseen delays and detours, not all of which had been caused by nature. On those occasions it had taken all of Matt's dexterity with his fists and six-gun to set them back on the right trail again. While he wasn't a shootist by trade, he'd been in more than his share of gunfights.

Matt Sutton was a cowboy from West Texas who had fallen in with bad company and had run afoul of the law, but he'd paid for it and was now starting over, a much wiser and more sober man. Tall, tanned, ruggedly handsome and rawhide lean, with shaggy brown hair, alert grey eyes that held a positive self-certainty, he looked all of his twenty-eight years and then some. His clothes were plain and comfortable: dove-grey, flat-crowned hat, yellow neckerchief, buckskin jacket, red and yellow checked flannel work shirt, soft, faded denims, scuffed boots, and a low-slung, holstered Colt .45 on his shell-belt that looked lethal and well-used.

In stark contrast, his companion looked and dressed like a thoroughbred. Diana Logan was an exquisite beauty, with high, explicit cheekbones, large, wide-spaced blue eyes, classic nose, softly moulded lips, firm chin, and cascading honey-gold hair that framed her delicate features. At twenty-six, she looked no more than nineteen, and her clothes emphasized her magnificent, willowy and statuesque figure.

Open low at her slender neck, which was wrapped by a long, narrowly folded white scarf, the thin white cotton shirt fit snugly, as did the short, fringed, soft, black leather jacket and short matching riding skirt that smoothly spanned her slim hips and clung to her taut thighs. Black gloves, matching flat-crowned hat with a silver hatband and thin chin cord, and 'peewees', a short and dressy pair of lighter weight, high-heeled boots, completed her outfit.

Diana was a gambler by trade, an occupation circumstances had forced upon her after the late War and its aftermath, the Reconstruction, had bled Texas and the rest of the Southern Confederacy.

Leaving the more genteel East Texas bayou country, she had travelled to the South-West frontier territories of New Mexico and Arizona, where she'd met Matt Sutton. Later she'd stuck by him when he was sent to prison for robbery, and now that he was out, they were going to make a new life together in California.

It was late afternoon when Matt noticed the huge storm cloud rolling in from the north and drew in his dun gelding. Dark and ominous, it was racing straight at them.

'How much time do we have?' Diana asked, concern in her throaty, velvet voice, as she halted her bay mare beside him.

'Not near long enough,' he answered grimly. She sighed her annoyance at the prospect of being drenched and turned in the saddle to untie the yellow slicker rolled up behind its cantle. 'No,' Matt snapped, and pointed across a vast sweep of grey distance that lay open before a thick forest of pine and aspen and the hills beyond. 'Ride like Lucifer himself was at your heels, and don't stop for nothing.' With that he swatted her horse's rump and sent it bolting forward. Always trying to take the lead, his dun needed no urging to head after the racing mare.

Only scant minutes passed till the storm was on them, darkening the sky and showering hail that became larger and harder as it continued to fall thickly. Their clothing gave little protection from the pelting stones which stung like fury and raised welts when they hit. Vivid flashes of lightning split the dark sky and thunderclaps rolled across the prairie. Eyes tearing, bodies smarting, the riders crouched lower in their saddles, not only to present smaller targets to the relentlessly pounding hail but to the stray lightning bolts, which were known to be drawn to the highest point in any area.

The first fury of the storm exhausted itself and the hail seemed to let up for a brief time. Still, the protecting timber lay several miles ahead. Determined to take advantage of the lull, Matt and Diana rein-whipped their staggering mounts into faster gallops. Side by side, watching each other from the corners of their eyes, they tore across the white hail-covered prairie, while above the anvil-blows of thunder built with the flickering lightning.

Then the hail returned with a vengeance, coming down harder than ever. Some stones were now the size of eggs and bounced high when they struck the ground with loud thumps. One grazed the side of Matt's head and left him seeing stars and flares and clinging to the pommel to brace himself. Diana cried out as a stone bruised her side and nearly broke a rib.

Ahead the trees loomed like dark spectres. The two were only yards away when a sliver of lightning jagged down to strike the top of a towering pine with a splitting, crackling explosion. Branches flew like scattered matchsticks as a flaming line parted the trunk to the ground and turned it into a bright beacon. Urgently controlling their frightened, rearing horses, the riders cut quickly from a straight course into a sharp, right-angle turn as flames leaped to the leaves and surrounding limbs of nearby trees.

With a crashing of brush Matt and Diana plunged

into the sheltering forest. Branches lashed against their faces and bodies as they wound between huge pine boles and slender aspens, whose madly fluttering leaves added to the racket. Thick, spreading limbs deflected most of the hail and lessened the hurt of the few ricocheting stones that found their mark. Clouds of eye-stinging grey smoke pursued them from the popping and crackling, flame-engulfed trees and their carpets of pine-needle litter.

Suddenly, as if in frustration, the hail stopped and the sky disgorged a furious volley of wind and rain. Thunder rumbled and cobweb patterns of lightning lit the black sky like day. Then darkness swept down again, and was all the more blinding in contrast, forcing the couple to tight-rein their horses and manoeuvre at a discreet pace through the woods.

By chance they came upon a game trail that led tortuously between the heavily dripping walls of dark, bordering trees. Behind them the increasing deluge appeared to have extinguished the burning trees before a full-fledged forest fire could erupt. Though the danger was past for the moment, they pushed on, with only a brief pause to dig out their rolled up slickers. Still, cold needles of rain pricked their faces as gusty winds wailed through the woods and gave the damp air the chill of winter.

Soon the slicker-shrouded pair lost track of time as they continued to prudently hold their horses to a slow, monotonous lope. Overhead, trees thrashed their branches and groaned in the onslaught of the icy wind, while lightning and thunder kept up their sight and sound imitation of a fireworks celebration.

Shivering, teeth chattering involuntarily, the two rode hunched in the saddle. The cold slickers had no inner linings and the dampness worked under their upturned collars, further soaking their already wet clothing and chilling them to the bone.

The timber became sparse and patchy, and they finally broke from the forest out on to an open flat which had been turned into a slithering sea of mud. They sat their horses and stared through the smoky downpour at a range of bush-cloaked hills a hundred yards ahead. A lightning display revealed a wide-mouthed cave bisecting one of the steep hillsides, and the two were heartened by the thought of the dryness that lay within. As though mocking their failure to immediately take advantage of such obvious shelter, the rain came sluicing down in cold, wind-driven sheets. Matt nodded to Diana and, head bowed to avoid the rain's sting, led the way across the mud-oozing flat.

The couple put their horses under a broad, rocky overhang that shelved the gaping entrance and hauled their gear wearily inside the cave. Leaving Diana to gather dry sticks and wood lying inside the cave's mouth, Matt trudged back out to unsaddle and tend to the horses.

Her search for firewood took Diana further back into the wide, deep cave. It was then that she sensed someone's presence there in the darkness, watching her every move. Listening intently, she strained to peer through the enveloping blackness. Then a dark shape separated itself from the shadows. Dropping her armload of sticks, she shrank away, a scream rising into her throat.

But it went unheard, for at that exact moment an ear-shattering thunderclap broke echoingly over the hills, and once more the rain redoubled its fury.

The horses brushed, grained, and hobbled for the night, Matt Sutton lugged the two saddles into the cave and halted in mid-stride. There was no fire and no sign of Diana. He was about to call to her when, out of the corner of his eye, he abruptly caught a glimpse of a glinting object swinging down at him. He released the saddles and tried to throw up an arm to ward it off but was too slow.

Something hard and cold smashed against his head and, agony ripping through his brain, he sank into a deep, black pit.

CHAPTER TWO

Something cold and wet was trailing gently over his face, and its soothing touch slowly restored Matt to consciousness. He had no idea how long he'd been lying there, but the rain was still pounding down outside and its noise was doing his fierce headache no good. Inside there was an almost cosy warmth, and the savoury odours of coffee and stew bubbling on a blazing fire.

Matt heard a soft, familiar voice speaking to him, in a tender yet urgent tone, and realized his throbbing head was resting in Diana's lap. He opened his eyes and saw only a pale, indistinct shape outlined by a thick yellow mass. Then his sight cleared and he stared up into Diana's beautiful, concerned face, her flowing blonde hair masking one blue eye.

'Matt,' she whispered hoarsely, 'are you all right?' It seemed like she wanted to say more but was afraid.

Unable to get his tongue working right, Matt managed the semblance of a smile and hoped it was reassuring. As she removed the wet cloth from his forehead, he noticed curiously that she now wore her brief, black gambling outfit. The low-cut, one-piece theatrical costume, with a corseted waist, fish-net stockings, and slender French heels revealed plenty of legs and cleavage and were intended to distract a player from his card game. He figured she'd changed while her wet clothes were drying. But then he also saw that her slim wrists were crossed and roped together, and the sight jogged his groggy brain and brought back the memory of what had happened.

He gave a start and tried to sit up, only to find he was tied hand and foot, with his arms behind his back. The headache, which he'd momentarily forgotten, vehemently reminded him of its presence by sending an agonizing pain streaking through his head, and he sank back, sharply sucking air through hard-clenched teeth.

'You see, ma'am, you fretted for nothin',' a quiet voice drawled pleasantly. 'That tap on the head weren't near hard enough to do any real bad hurt.'

Wincing with the effort, Matt turned his head to see a tall man, wolf-lean, in his late thirties, dressed similarly to him, sitting cross-legged on the other side of the fire, where coffee and a pot of stew were cooking, and Diana's clothes spread on a nearby saddle. The flickering flames threw shadows over his long, homely face, netted with seams and creases of years in the open, and black beard stubble that matched his eyes and straight, unkempt hair.

'Pretty good fit, huh?' the stranger remarked, and nodded down at his clothes.

Disregarding the wrenching pain that shot down through his neck and spine, Matt struggled to a half-sitting position, braced up on an elbow, and looked at himself. For a moment his head spun and his vision blurred. Then it cleared and he saw the unfamiliar clothing: faded, well-worn denims, grey wool shirt, and a pair of half boots more scuffed than his own.

'I swapped with you whilst you was sleepin',' the tall man explained. 'And before you go gittin' riled, the lady changed herself, back there in the dark.' He jerked a thumb towards the blackness in the rear of the cave, then grinned and said with disarming candour, 'I did put forth the suggestion that she'd look more fetchin' in that than anythin' else she had in her saddle-bags, and that it'd make passin' a rainy night more pleasant.'

His words met only hostile silence. Undaunted, he continued in seemingly genuine regret, 'I'm sorry to do you folks like this, but there's a hanging party after me for somethin' I did *not* do.' He deliberately paused and poured himself a cup of steaming coffee. Neither prisoner expressed an interest in his tale. 'They come on my camp just before dawn and started accusin', then shootin', without givin' me a chance to explain. I held 'em off, then made a break, and give 'em the slip whilst it was still dark. Bullet got my horse but he carried me a-ways before expirin'. Been walkin' since late mornin'. I found this place just as the storm was fixin' to cut loose, and a short time afterwards you two showed up.'

'What do you want from us?' Matt asked thickly.

'To share your victuals,' he replied simply. 'And the loan of one of your horses when this storm's over.'

14

'Horse-stealing is a hanging offence,' Matt said.

The gaunt man shrugged casually. 'I surely will hang if I wait around here for that posse.'

'What are you accused of doing?' Diana asked coldly.

'Seems a rancher's wife over in Willow Creek was misused and kilt.' He saw the shock and fear on Diana's face and added quickly, 'I done a lotta things I ain't right proud of – but I ain't a killer – 'specially of women.'

'Why do they think it was you?' Matt asked.

'Somebody claims to have seen me leavin' there. I admit bein' at the ranch and choppin' firewood for a meal and some food to take with me. I done that lotsa places. Been ridin' the grub line for near six months now.' He took a sip of coffee and eyed Diana. 'She was pretty – not near as much as you, ma'am – but I never touched her. And even if I'd had such impure thoughts I still wouldn't have, 'cause she was in a family way.'

Matt and Diana were appalled. Both were Texans and Southerners, and the murder of a pregnant woman was deemed a heinous act indeed. Throughout the frontier women were scarce and therefore accorded great respect. Even a damn yankee behaved as chivalrous as a Southern cavalier around a woman. Not pestering a woman was the one rule that was rarely ever broken, and a man guilty of rape or murder would be hanged immediately from the nearest tree.

'I got no idea who done her. Might have been her own man for all I know,' the gaunt man said solemnly. 'But I do know that it's always a lot easier and more comfortin' for folks to blame such a deed on a drifter than admit that a friend or neighbour is a killer.'

'Maybe so,' Matt agreed noncommittally.

'Besides, you know how most posses work. They catch a fella, figure it's too much bother to bring him in, then take time off from ranching and such to ride back and forth for the trial – and there's always the chance the judge won't see things their way. No, they'd as lief judge and execute him right on the spot. Many an innocent man has met that fate.'

'So have a lot of guilty ones,' Matt put in flatly.

The gaunt man paid him no heed. 'Anyways, that's why I'm lightin' a shuck outta Utah Territory.' His dark eyes slowly swept the captives' faces. 'Now you just behave yourselves and we'll git along like home-folks till I leave.'

'In my clothes,' Matt said evenly.

'Nobody's lookin' for a fella in these duds – 'less'n you done somethin' shameful you ain't tol' me about?'

'And if we run into that trigger-happy posse and I'm in these clothes, they'll take me for you.'

'That's the general idea. 'Course, you got the lady with you, and she oughta help sort things out.'

'Providing we're given the chance to speak.'

'We all gotta take chances in this cruel ol' world.'

'Would you untie us,' Diana asked, letting even more of the South come provocatively into her throaty, velvet voice, 'if we gave our word to be on our best behaviour?'

16

The man grinned knowingly. 'My mama didn't raise no idiot child.' He saw the blue lightning flash in Diana's big eyes at his rejection, then looked down at the stew. 'Supper is ready. I'll eat first, then the lady, and then she can feed you.'

'Tie my hands in front and I'll feed myself.'

'You'll stay like you are. You oughta be happy havin' such a fine-lookin' gal waitin' on you.'

With that the gaunt man dished out a heaping plate of stew and set upon it ravenously while Matt and Diana watched in silence. Outside the rain and thunder continued without let-up, along with sporadic lightning. When the man had finished and relaxed over his coffee, he called Diana to him. Rising gracefully, in spite of her high heels and tied hands, she went to the fire, where he freed her and had her sit and eat. Then Diana took coffee and a plate of food to Matt, who squirmed to a sitting position, and hand-fed him under their captor's watchful eye.

The warmth and the meal took their toll and soon all three were trying unsuccessfully to stifle yawns. Matt's knots were checked and his oilskin slicker was slung over him so its rustling would betray any movement, however slight, that he made during the night. Diana flashed the gaunt man an arctic scowl as, slipping off her shoes and stretching out on the blanket on her stomach, her crossed wrists and ankles were bound securely and joined together by a separate rope in a loose hog-tie. Another blanket was draped over her body, then her captor moved off, collected the messware, and set it out to soak just beyond the cave's entrance. He sat down to wait in the mouth of the cave and stared out into the steadily falling rain that danced musically in the rapidly filling pans.

Impatiently, Matt shammed sleep until the gaunt man finally brought the messware back inside, stood briefly over each captive, then, satisfied that they were asleep, crawled into his own blankets that were positioned so he could see both prisoners at once. After what seemed an eternity but was actually less than half an hour, the man fell into a deep sleep. Still, Matt gave it ten more minutes before straining against his ropes, contracting then relaxing his muscles, attempting to twist his crossed wrists about inside their tight coils, fingers probing for the elusive knot.

Whenever sleep overtook Matt, it was against his will, then he'd be awake, immediately pitting himself against the ropes again. It was a waste of time and effort. He was forced to work too cautiously, unable to really move much because of the damn noisy slicker. Frustrated, he at last fell into an exhausted sleep from which he was unable to rouse himself.

CHAPTER THREE

Rafe Lonis woke just before dawn. He sat up suddenly, as if he thought someone was slipping up on him. A hasty glance revealed that the captives were asleep in their places. Sliding his six-gun from its holster beside him on the ground, he tossed off his blanket, then stood and moved to the mouth of the cave where he could look out.

A grey, steady rain was falling. It streamed in silvery torrents off the rocks and ledges. Lonis stepped out and stood under the rocky overhang. The horses were huddled off to one side, still in their hobbles, and no posse was sneaking out of the woods after him. There was no danger at all. It was just something in the air that made him uneasy.

Why shouldn't he be uneasy? He wasn't used to being a hunted man, running for his life like a scared jack-rabbit. If it had been a crime of his own doing that was one thing, but he sure as hell hated to die for something that, this time, he did not have a hand in. Fate had led him to that damn ranch and straight into this mess, and it was now up to fate to do right by him.

The dark, miserable morning matched Lonis's mood. Then a faint orange streak mixed with the grey-black eastern sky, announced that the rain shouldn't hang around too much longer, and that knowledge brought Lonis a clarity of mind. He now knew what he had to do. He didn't like himself too much for it, but he couldn't afford a conscience when his own life was at stake. His mind set, he turned and went back into the cave.

Matt was so exhausted that he only stirred but did not awaken at the sounds of movement about the cave. It was only later, when the crackling oilskin was pulled from him, that he woke. His sleep-slick eyes stared up at his captor, who stood over him shrugging into the noisy slicker.

'I'm goin',' the man announced. 'I'm leavin' you my old slicker and warbags,' he motioned towards his saddle-bags near the smouldering ashes that remained of the night's fire.

'Where's Diana?' Matt asked, his mouth feeling like cotton.

'Outside waitin' for me,' the man said solemnly. 'She's my insurance. The posse's lookin' for a lone man, not a man and woman travelling together. And if'n they catch you and you manage to persuade 'em you ain't me, then she'll make a right useful hostage.'

'You cowardly son of a—'

'Now don't go to cussin' me, or I'm liable to break my word to her and boot your head so hard your brains will be mush.' He leaned closer. 'I truly don't

20

plan her no hurt, and soon as I'm safe I'll leave her tied within walkin' distance of the nearest ranch or town we come upon. By the time she's got herself loose and walked there, I'll be long gone.'

'Wherever you go I'll find you.'

'That's mighty big talk for a man with no horse or gun, and a blood-mad posse huntin' him.'

'I'm not talking lightly,' Matt said, meeting his eyes coldly, 'it's a promise.'

'Long as she's with me,' Lonis said, his eyes boring right back against Matt's hard stare, 'you'd best keep your damn distance, for her well-bein' – and that's a promise.' He turned on a boot-heel and, slicker rustling, strode back to the mouth of the cave, then paused and looked back.

'The rain's startin' to let up,' Lonis announced, almost conversationally, 'and that posse'll be roamin' around this way.' He grinned sardonically. 'You'll understand if I don't wish you good luck.' With that he went out, slicker flapping.

Matt lay there stewing in angry frustration. The tall man was right. It looked as though he didn't stand a Chinaman's chance, but he and Diana had faced almost hopeless odds before and had come out all right. And by the Lord Harry, he was determined that they would do so again.

Wearing her hat and slicker, which was draped over her scantily clad figure, Diana sat shivering on her hobbled horse under the dripping overhang. Her wrists and arms were tied behind her and her high-heeled feet were shoved into her stirrups and held

21

there by ropes about her trim, fish-net stockinged ankles. Eyes wide above her white scarf gag, she divided her attention apprehensively between the mouth of the cave and the rain-soaked landscape, with an early morning fog drifting eerily through the glistening woods.

There was no sign of the posse. Had the rain washed away the man's tracks, forcing the posse to give up and return to town? If not, she wished they would hurry up and arrive before she was forced to leave with her abductor. Then she would be able to explain clearly who was whom, despite the men's change of clothes.

Diana tensed, hands knotting into tight balls, as the tall man emerged from the cave buttoning a crackling slicker, which she recognized as Matt's.

'I done like I said,' Lonis reassured her. He knelt and removed the horse's hobbles, then stuffed them into a pocket of Diana's saddle-bags, slung behind the cantle with her bedroll. 'He can git loose if'n he has sense to burn them ropes before the fire dies out completely.' He moved to his horse, repeated the process, then mounted and took the dangling reins of Diana's mare.

As she was led out into the cold, drizzling rain, Diana craned her neck to look back at the cave and tried to convince herself that somehow Matt would find her. She clung desperately to that hope.

Less than fifteen minutes after hearing Lonis leave with Diana, Matt Sutton had succeeded in freeing himself. It had entailed a painful, crab-like crawl to the dying fire, and cautiously burning through his wrist ropes without doing too much damage to himself. A sweep of the cave had yielded Lonis's frayed denim jumper, battered, high-peaked hat, patched, well-used slicker, with a red bandanna inside one pocket, and empty saddle-bags, which he left.

He now stood under the granite overhang and surveyed the area about him. The rain had become a fine mist. The early morning sky was fast losing its gloom and giving way to bright sunlight. Visible in the mire, the horses' tracks led off towards the north-west but the riders were already out of sight. Matt hesitated and debated his next move.

There was no telling how long it would be before the posse came this way. Also, there was no guarantee they would even believe him, despite his cut and bruised wrists and the two horses' trail – particularly if they were indeed trigger-happy like the tall man had claimed. He decided that his best bet was to follow the tracks and worry about the posse when and if they came upon him.

Buttoning the slicker and pulling down the hat's wide, curving brim, Matt stepped out into the mist and his boots sank instantly into the muddy slime. Careful not to disrupt the hoofprints so that the posse could follow, he began plodding through the muck that sucked at his boots with every step he took.

Some long miles off to the south-east, the morning sun was baking the earth dry. Led by Deputy Sheriff

Andy Denham, a slim, pleasant-faced man of twenty-seven, the fifteen-man posse from Willow Creek sat their shying mounts and stared sombrely at the ghastly remains of Lonis's dead horse, badly ripped apart by the big, ugly, black turkey buzzards that hovered high above, screeching impatiently for the intruders to leave so they could finish their interrupted meal.

'He done left his hull behind,' redheaded 'Brick' Calloway exclaimed derisively, expressing a 'puncher's widely held belief that even a down-on-his-luck cowboy should never sell or abandon his saddle, as it meant he was financially or morally 'in the depths'. It was his work bench, his pride, his throne, and without it he felt degraded.

'Well, I'd say he didn't have much choice,' commented Amos Long, a paunchy, middle-aged man in a black town suit.

Calloway gave him an irritated glance and shook his head. 'I wouldn't expect no store-keeper to understand.' He smirked as several other ranch hands piped up in agreement.

'Now he's afoot we oughta ride him down before the day's half out,' one of the men said confidently.

'If he hasn't gone to ground and holed up in one of the many caves in those distant mountains,' put in town lawyer Jesse Seaton, a handsome, dark-haired man in his early thirties.

Andy Denham nodded. 'It would take a lotta hunting to dig him out.'

'I'll follow him to the depths of hell,' stated Elijah Hobson, the burly, greying, grim-featured husband of the murdered young woman.

'Are you talking about quitting?' demanded Wesley Trask, a lean, cocky, flashily dressed young man with a two holster rig, causing some of the others, mostly town loafers and saloon soldiers, to set up a commotion. Then his father, Hiram Trask, a rugged, middle-aged rancher who controlled most of Willow Creek, made another of his bids to lead.

'If you're not up to the job, Denham, head on back to town and we'll take care of this ourselves.'

The deputy was sorely tempted to do just that. He hadn't wanted this chore to begin with. Until only a few days ago Willow Creek had been a sleepy little town where the only excitement was an occasional Saturday night brawl. Naturally as soon as Sheriff Crandall was laid low with a bad case of pneumonia, all hell chose to break loose.

Amiable and content with his status, Andy Denham had always considered himself a follower and was ill at ease in this new position of leadership that had been thrust upon him. Still, he wasn't going to let Crandall down by allowing the posse to degenerate into a mindless lynch mob if he could help it.

Andy held up a hand for silence and made his tone friendly yet firm. 'I ain't empowered to swear anybody in as a deputy, only Sheriff Crandall can do that. As long as I'm with you the law is represented, otherwise you're no better than—'

'Save it, Deputy,' Wesley Trask interrupted sarcastically. 'We have lawyer Seaton here who can serve as a judge, and more than enough men for a jury. That makes us more legal than most posses hereabouts.'

The saloon toughs and 'punchers from his father's ranch eagerly seconded Trask's words. Andy looked to the lawyer for support, and Seaton understood his wordless plea.

'May I remind everyone that the accused man first has to be caught,' Seaton said smoothly. 'So I suggest we stop this bickering, get away from the stench of that horse and those screeching birds, and search for any footprints that haven't been washed away by the rain.'

Emboldened by the stillness of the horsemen, one huge, bloated buzzard swooped down towards the fly-covered carcass. In a quick, fluid movement Wes Trask drew his Colt .45 and fired a single, echoing shot. Showering feathers, the turkey buzzard somersaulted in the air, then plummeted to the ground with a thump, and flopped around for a long moment in its death throes before going limp. Screaming and calling noisily, the other carrion birds climbed higher and retreated a short distance, then resumed their lazy circles.

'That was some shootin', Wes,' Brick Calloway praised. Like the typical 'puncher, he did very little shooting, as bullets were expensive and his pay was only a dollar a day. Besides, ranch work left no time for the ceaseless hours of practice required to become a fast-draw artist.

Wes beamed. 'Reckon that took care of a bit of the noise.' He returned the gun to its holster with a fancy twirl. But his pride in his accomplishment was short-lived.

'It was a senseless waste of cartridges,' said the

elder Trask curtly. 'That shot carried for miles, and told the man we're after our whereabouts.' Disregarding his son's hang-dog expression as Wes appeared to wilt in his saddle, Hiram Trask cast a sweeping glance about the bleak area and added, 'He's going to be even more careful now.'

'It was an honest mistake, Hiram,' Jesse Seaton said, trying to smooth things over.

'I don't need you to plead my case,' Wes snapped sullenly.

Andy saw his chance and jumped in, asserting his fragile control over the group. 'All right, let's spread out and start hunting. The damage has already been done, so go on ahead and fire one shot if you find his trail, and three if you spot him. Remember, don't try to take him by yourself. Wait till the rest of us get there.'

Before the deputy had even finished Wes Trask put his big-rowelled spurs to his paint gelding and galloped off with some of the whooping 'punchers. The rest waited and then dispersed at a more leisurely pace.

Andy hung back and stared after the scattering posse. He was determined that the fugitive would not give them the slip again. Exactly what would happen when they finally caught up with him was anybody's guess. If the man was taken alive Andy knew he could count on Seaton, Amos Long and a few of the other reputable townsfolk to remain cool-headed and refuse to go along with a necktie party. Of course it would be a whole lot easier for all concerned if the man died in a gunbattle. It would be a nice, clean ending, with nobody having to choose sides.

Then an unsettling thought came to Andy. Suppose Orin Fowle, Hobson's nearest neighbour, was wrong in his claim of seeing the man riding from the ranch? Fowle was a surly, grizzled man who ran a small horse ranch and pretty much kept his own company. Though he wasn't much liked, Fowle was considered honest, sober, and hard-working. Still, even the most upright citizen could make a mistake. And that mistake could be fatal to an innocent man.

As he watched Fowle's ramrod-straight figure riding off away from the others, Andy again reminded himself that his job was to bring the fugitive in for the circuit judge to preside over. It wasn't his job to decide the man's guilt or innocence, or to even serve on a jury, for that matter.

Holding that comforting thought, Andy gigged his horse with his spurs and rode away, leaving the squawking buzzards to descend and finish their meal in peace.

CHAPTER FOUR

The mid-morning sun beat down on the two slicker-clad riders cantering across the prairie. Though the rain had ended some time ago Rafe Lonis continued to push on without even a halt to remove their rain gear. The stifling slicker was causing Diana to perspire, adding to her other discomforts. The gag dried her mouth and pinched her cheeks and the ropes numbed her wrists, arms and ankles. She was relieved when her captor, who held her horse's reins, finally slowed and, cinches creaking against the clop of their mounts' hoofs, swivelled in the saddle to survey the wide expanse that they were crossing.

Satisfied that there was no one in sight, Lonis drew up, smiled over at Diana, and announced, 'We'll stop a spell and let the horses blow.' He released her reins, swung from the saddle and lowered himself heavily to the ground, where he shrugged out of his slicker and tied it behind his cantle. Stretching and rubbing his lower back, he moved to Diana and freed one ankle, then the other from her stirrups.

Diana didn't resist as Lonis helped her down. To her chagrin, her long legs were numb and she fell

29

heavily against his chest. Plainly enjoying their close-
ness, he grinned widely and held her until she
regained her equilibrium, then she stiffened and
wrenched out of his arms, staggering in her high
heels on the uneven ground.

'Just settle down and I'll git you outta that old
fish,' Lonis said amiably, using a cowboy term for the
yellow oilskin slicker. Blue eyes baleful, Diana held
her ground as he approached her, as carefully as he
would a skittish colt. He undid the two buttons which
held the slicker in place, slid it from about her bare
shoulders and dropped it to the ground. As he did,
he couldn't help but notice that her tied arms drew
her shoulders back sharply and caused her firm,
sweat-glistening breasts to thrust brazenly between
their surrounding ropes and against the low top of
her black costume.

Diana followed her captor's gaze and went rigid,
meeting his eyes with cold indignation; to show fear
might well invite disaster. Despite her predicament
she must not acknowledge her true helplessness at
any time.

'It don't hurt none to look,' Lonis said unabashed.
He made a twirling motion with one hand. 'Now turn
around and I'll take off your gag and ropes for a bit.'

Diana eyed Lonis warily but complied, and he
loosened the scarf and drew it down to hang slackly
about her graceful neck. She sighed her relief and
worked her jaw while he fumbled with the tight knots
holding her ropes. He stepped back with the ropes
and she turned to face him, wincing as she chafed
her aching, deeply marked wrists gingerly.

'Soon as you're able,' Lonis said, watching indifferently, 'put on your ridin' duds.'

Diana looked up from her wrists in mock amazement. 'I thought you preferred me like this?' she said, her throaty voice dripping sarcasm.

'I surely do,' Lonis replied, 'but you'll attract less attention the other way.'

Diana motioned about the desolate, treeless expanse. 'There is no place to change in private.'

'Go behind your horse. I won't look.' He saw her dubious expression and added, 'I ain't about to close my eyes or turn around so's you can crown me with a rock and then ride off, leavin' me high and dry.'

Diana smiled maliciously at the thought and continued chafing her throbbing wrists. 'I refuse to undress as long as we are on this prairie.'

'Then put your things on over that outfit,' Lonis compromised, 'but take off them stockings and French heels.'

Diana turned haughtily, dug her clothes from a bulging saddle-bag pouch, then went around to the other side of her horse and began to dress.

For some time Matt Sutton had maintained a steady, mile-eating pace, dog-trotting one hundred feet, then walking the next hundred, but he was now tiring. The late morning sun was draining his endurance, growing hotter by the minute and bringing a thirst he was unable to quench, as it crept towards its zenith in the cloudless sky.

Matt halted, thumbed the hat back off his forehead, and stood gasping for breath while wiping salty

31

sweat from his stinging eyes with a sleeve of his jumper. Miles back, he'd discarded the cumbersome slicker as soon as the weather had cleared. Pulling the red bandanna from his back pocket, he wiped the sweatband of his hat dry as he stared down at the still visible and fairly fresh hoofprints.

The man was pushing it and still leading Diana's horse behind him, varying the pace from a fast trot to a gallop. Not knowing the country and unaware of any short cut, Matt had no hope of catching up without a horse. Any scant distance Matt might gain whenever the man stopped to let the horses blow would be lost the moment he started off again. But that didn't mean he was calling it quits and waiting for the posse – not by a long shot.

Stuffing the bandanna into a pocket and placing the hat low on his forehead, Matt stooped to pick up a pebble and pop it under his tongue. It was an old Indian trick to help keep the inside of one's mouth from becoming dry. Sucking on the pebble, Matt, legs aching, set off towards a group of hills some distance ahead.

Wes Trask held in his skittish, side-stepping paint and stared down at the cast off slicker, flapping and rustling in the wind like a large, stomped-flat yellow critter. The trail remained the same as he'd been following since leaving the cave. The fugitive still dogged the two riders, one a woman, who, evidently intimidated by their brush with him in the cave, continued at a relentless pace.

Again Wes did not fire a signal shot. Still smarting

from his father's censure in front of the whole posse, he was determined to ride the hunted man down by himself and show one and all he was worth his salt. Giving the slicker a wide go-round, he resumed following the trail.

Some miles back, Deputy Andy Denham and the rest of the posse rode away from the cave and continued their pursuit. Andy was irked that once more Wes Trask was trying to show off, having come and gone without firing a signal shot and then waiting for the posse to catch up. Briefly, Andy took petty delight in the thought that the cocky, annoying bully might just bite off more than he could chew.

As the group jogged along, some of the ranch hands speculated about the woman's looks. It was apparent that a couple had taken shelter from the storm inside the cave and had run afoul of the outlaw. Judging by the burned rope beside the remains of a fire, they had captured the fugitive and left him for the posse. But he had freed himself and, seeking a horse, headed after them on foot.

Andy wasn't completely sure he went along with that story, but he did have to admit the footprints were made by the same boots they'd been following ever since the man had lost his horse. The only way to learn for sure would be to catch up with the man. That shouldn't be too much longer now, and Andy was still more than a mite concerned about what would happen then.

Diana sat staring down at her tied, black-gloved

hands as Lonis attached them to her saddle horn with a short cinch rope. He made the knots tight, placed the reins into her hands and stepped away.

'Now you can guide your horse yourself,' he said pleasantly, 'and I got both my hands free for other things.'

Diana made no reply; at least the gloves gave some small protection from the chafing ropes, as did her boots with the ropes fastening her ankles to the stirrups. She now wore her shirt and riding skirt over her gambling costume and had removed her stockings. The scarf was still loose about her neck, ready to be drawn up as a gag should her captor see fit.

Lonis hauled himself up into the saddle and looked over at Diana. 'Keep by my side, and don't go gittin' no funny ideas.' She glowered at him from beneath her hat brim. 'I mean it now,' he cautioned sternly. 'Don't trifle with my good nature, or I'll thump you a good 'un.' He nudged his mount forward, and Diana followed obediently alongside.

As they rode at a fast trot, Diana threw a glance hopefully over her slim shoulder at the empty expanse behind them. There was still no sign of Matt, or the posse. She turned back and pondered dejectedly. Each mile was taking her further from Matt, and there was nothing she could do.

Diana bit her soft lip and continued fretting. Perhaps the man, who had finally identified himself as Rafe Lonis, would grow careless, or his horse might step in a prairie dog hole, and then she would have a chance to escape. Even though she was tied, she could still ride until she encountered help.

34

Cheered by that thought, Diana set her mind to scheming how to use her womanly wiles to lull Lonis into a sense of trust without appearing obvious.

It was a fluke accident. A rock shifted beneath Matt's boot as he laboured up a hill, throwing him to his knees. At that instant he felt a strong rush of air above his head, then dirt and grass kicked up in his face, and he heard the flat ugly crack of a distant rifle. Immediately he threw himself down and lay still, shamming being hit. He was too exposed and the shooter was too good a marksman for Matt to risk trying to scramble the remaining yards that would take him over the crest. Cursing his carelessness, he waited, listening to the galloping hoofbeats.

Wes Trask grinned in triumph. He had redeemed his pride by taking the outlaw all by himself; neither his old man nor anybody else could fault him now. The shot should have finished the man, but if not, the rifle was too awkward for up close work. He shoved it back into its boot, then drew one six-gun as he put his paint up the steep hill.

Hand resting on a fist-size clod of earth, Matt heard the rider struggle up towards him. His heart-beat pounding in his ears threatened to deafen him to the horse's approach, and he cracked his eyelids. He saw the rider, pistol in hand, slide back low in his saddle as the horse worked its way cautiously up the slope, making quick-footed recoveries in the loose dirt. Steeling himself, Matt rolled suddenly, sat up and hurled the clod at the horse's shoulder.

The paint let out a startled whinny and reared

high, almost toppling over. Caught by surprise Wes somersaulted backwards from the saddle. The Colt discharged into the air and leaped from his hand. He slammed to the ground and tumbled dizzily down the hillside in a huge cloud of dust and debris, losing his other pistol from its holster. Breath driven from his body, he lay dazed, pinwheels of pain spinning brightly before his eyes.

Matt was on his feet as the frightened horse started to lunge past. Grabbing the dangling reins in one hand and the pommel in the other, he swung up into the saddle, brought the animal under control, then halted at the summit and threw a backwards glance. He was relieved to see his attacker sprawled ungainly at the foot of the hill.

Ahead stretched a desolate prairie with no sign of movement upon it. The horse meant a good chance of now catching up with Diana and her captor before the posse, which would make explaining things a whole lot easier. He nudged the paint forward and headed down the hill.

Wes Trask's distant rifle shot had reached Andy Denham's ears and he'd then summoned the strung-out posse together with a shot of his own. Now there was hurried speculation about what had happened. Some were in hopes that Wes had ended the hunt while others, who were looking forward to being in on the kill, were disappointed at the thought. Again, Andy was in a secret turmoil about either outcome.

Then Wes's pistol shot interrupted further discussion and sent the posse galloping off in a body in the direction it had come.

Miles away and well out of earshot of the events taking place behind him, Rafe Lonis was lost in pleasurable contemplation, thinking long and hard about the yellow-haired beauty riding by his stirrup. Since she'd lost some of her surliness and was now being almost civil, how would she take it if'n he was to keep her with him? He wasn't all that much with the ladies, but being in her company sure boosted his self-esteem.

A fella who claimed to have been married a coupla-three times had once told him that training a woman was no different from training a horse. Keep a tight rein till she finally learns who's boss, then ease up a mite and be kinda gentle till she steps outta line. Yes siree-bob, he'd surely enjoy training Diana Logan.

Lonis's sidelong glance lingered on Diana's jouncing breasts, thrusting inside her snug shirt with each step of her trotting horse, and he couldn't help but let his thoughts turn a mite lewd. Then he was jolted from his musings by the close warning sound of a large rattlesnake as it drew its body up into a tight, hissing coil, tail rattling, deadly fanged jaws open wide.

Squealing in fright, his horse reared wildly, front legs climbing the air, then landed hard and sunfished, twisting his back and hindquarters. Unprepared, Lonis clung to the horn as he was flung sideways, half out of the saddle, and lost one rein.

Bawling and snorting chestily, the dun made several long crowhops that took it well away from the snake, then dropped its head and began to kick and buck.

Simultaneously, Diana's mare shied and danced away from both the snake and the bucking dun. This was the chance she had awaited, and she took full advantage of the situation. Wrenching the horse around, she booted it into a dead run. She knew she was risking life and limb: should her mount stumble or step into a prairie dog hole, she would go down under it. Still, there might not be another chance like this again.

Maintaining an all-out gallop, Diana continued back across the prairie and prayed desperately that she would encounter the posse before Lonis could regain control of his horse and ride her down.

CHAPTER FIVE

Lonis righted himself in the saddle and hung on tight. All he could do was stay aboard until the dun tired. Otherwise, he would be afoot again, which was something he couldn't afford. He'd caught a glimpse of his captive as she'd made her break, leaving him with the choice of running her down or else continuing on his way alone – providing he didn't get thrown.

From past ranch work, Lonis was fairly experienced with bucking broncs, and soon he was rocking back and forth in unison with the dun's frenzied movements. Then, abruptly, it was over. The dun stopped in his tracks, flanks heaving, nostrils blowing wind. Biting back his animosity, Lonis patted the horse's sweaty neck and spoke reassuringly while he caught up the loose rein.

The damn snake had gone to ground. It was just as well as there was no time to waste on petty revenge (as gratifying as that would have been), for his prisoner's shrinking image was riding hell-for-leather back across the prairie. He mulled over his options, decided that even though the girl was a hindrance she was still a useful hostage, and started after her at a strong, ground-eating lope.

Crouched low in the saddle of her racing horse, Diana dared a look back over her shoulder and saw Lonis rapidly closing the separating distance. Heart pounding, she turned and urged the mare on at an even more reckless gallop.

A hot anger began to boil in Lonis as he relentlessly put the dun into a wild run. Not only was the girl wasting precious time and causing him to backtrack, she was courting injury or death to both herself and her mount. A lost horse meant they would have to double up, which would slow him down considerably. An injury to herself would also slow him, unless he left her for the posse to find. And if she broke her damn fool neck, another murder would be pinned on him. He was sorely tempted to just leave her to her own devices, but his growing rage spurred him on.

Damn it all, he'd done warned her to act right, and she'd seen fit to disobey. Well, it was his own fault for treating her too nice. Whether or not he decided to keep her for his woman, it was high time for her first training lesson. He full intended to wallop her right smack into the middle of next week, and put the fear of God into her once and for all!

The riders thundered across the prairie, hearing only the wild tattoo of hoofs, and the wind of their breakneck speed tearing at their hats and clothing and roaring in their ears. Diana's hat flew back, hanging between her shoulders by its chin cord, and her long hair lashed stingingly at her face and eyes.

She heard her pursuer closing upon her and, though blinded by her teary eyes and spidery maze of loose hair, kept the mare at a full gallop, heedless of the danger.

Thick dust clouds marked the riders' passage as the chase raged mile after contested mile back across the prairie and away from the rugged, stairstep mountains that Lonis had been making for, hoping to hide their trail. Squinting through the billowing dust, Lonis stuck doggedly on his fleeing captive's tail. He was cutting the gap steadily but still unable to overtake her.

Then Diana's frothing, wheezing mount stumbled wearily on the uneven ground and started to go down. Frantically she yanked its head up as the horse floundered, and felt her ropes bite sharply into her slim wrists with the violent movement. That break in stride slowed her and gave Lonis the chance to finally draw alongside with a quick burst of speed. Diana started to veer her horse away but was too late.

Dust-grimy face a mask of fury, Lonis leaned over and slammed a hard fist into the hinge of her jaw. The force flung Diana sideways, and only her wrist and ankle ropes kept her in the saddle as she went limp as a rag doll, face buried in the mare's sweat-damp mane. Lonis caught her reins, drew both panting horses to a halt, and sat scowling down at the unconscious blonde while struggling to regain his composure. He couldn't rightly fault her for making a break, but he sure as hell could see to it that she didn't do so again.

*

Bravado waning, Wes Trask felt sweat from the noon-day sun trickle down his back as he looked about at the semi-circled horsemen. Their sceptical faces made plain that his tale about being surprised by the outlaw didn't hold water. For a change his father was strangely silent, but the shame and disappointment expressed on his jowly face stung Wes far more than the tongue-lashing Andy Denham was administering.

'Thanks to you the outlaw now has a horse and rifle, and a good lead on us. Instead of being over, this hunt is going on a lot longer than it should. If he makes it up into those mountains, he might get clean away.'

'That's Ute country,' Brick Calloway interjected, coming to Wes's aid. 'What's the difference between them scalping him or us hanging him, just so long as the job gets done?' Several other Trask 'punchers voiced their agreement, and he beamed widely and looked to Wes, whose spirits were lifted by his words.

'I didn't come along to scrap with no damn Utes,' said one of the saloon layabouts, who was instantly seconded by his companions.

'It won't come to that if we can catch him before he reaches the mountains,' Andy said sternly. 'Now let's ride.'

'Brick, gimme your horse,' Wes said, 'and you ride the pack horse till we run that jasper down.'

Seeing how the ranch supplied horses to its hands and Wes was the boss's son, Brick hid his displeasure and turned over his horse. This was a fine reward for him speaking up on Wes's behalf. He sure wasn't gonna extend himself again.

With Brick seated uncomfortably on the pack horse and bringing up the dusty rear, the posse resumed its grim hunt.

Matt Sutton got down stiffly from the saddle and stretched his tired legs while letting the paint blow. By the look of things Diana and her captor had stopped to rest for a spell and she'd changed clothes, since her bootprints had replaced those made by her French heels. He squinted off into the distance and could make out nothing but the shape of a mountain range looming at the prairie's end, which was evidently where the fugitive was headed. A look behind showed no sign of the posse, but sure as the sun was shining it was back there somewheres, following his trail.

Aware that he shouldn't linger too long, Matt moved to the waiting horse. Leather cinches creaking, Matt hauled himself aboard, then kicked the paint into motion.

It was well past noon and the sun was scorching hot, further adding to Diana Logan's waking discomforts. Her jaw throbbed dully, her body was stiff and cramped, and the strong odour of horse filled her nostrils. Her head lolled from side to side with the mare's steady jogging, and she realized that her face was in the animal's scratchy, salt-stiffened mane. Something large and soft was wedged between her teeth, holding her mouth open wide, and from the tight parallel indentations she felt along her cheeks and the pressure at the base of her skull, she knew that she was gagged with her broadly knotted scarf.

As the vertigo and nausea diminished, Diana attempted to straighten up in the saddle but discovered that her arms were again bound behind her at the wrists and touching elbows. Ropes also encircled her breasts and midriff, and a separate length tautly attached her body to the pommel by her waist. She raised her head and saw through her wildly dishevelled hair that her reins were tied to the end of a long rope which was affixed to Lonis's saddle horn.

Slouched loosely in the saddle, the tall man seemed oblivious to Diana's waking as he led the way through a jumble of rocks, barren of any growth except for an occasional piñon or yucca, and started the climb into the foothills to the towering mountains beyond. The sharp grade raised the mare's forequarters, and by leaning back in the saddle Diana was able to achieve an upright position. Lonis looked back sourly, saw that she was awake and her horse was having no difficulty ascending the steep slope, then stared out searchingly at the prairie below, shimmering madly in the afternoon heat. Satisfied there were no pursuers, he turned away and gave the narrowing switchback trail his full attention.

Wishing her hat were on her bare head instead of dangling down between her shoulder blades, Diana listened to the rhythmical clopping of the horses and tried to disregard the searing sun. Squinting against its glare, she sought to penetrate the dancing heat vapours. She knew that Matt was out there somewhere, and nothing was going to shake her belief.

Suddenly she tensed, eyes wide above her jaw-creaking gag, as she spotted the far distant figure of a single rider. Fearing it was a mirage brought on by a sun-addled brain, she blinked and shook her head, flinging away the beads of perspiration making their way down her brow and threatening to blind her momentarily with their stinging salt. Breath tight in her chest she looked again.

The image remained, moving slowly amid the wavering haze.

Relief flooded over Diana. While the horseman was too far away for her to be certain he was Matt, he still represented the hope of rescue. He might be a scout for the posse. She looked quickly to Lonis, whose attention was taken up with the twisting trail ahead, then back to the distant rider. Her smooth brow knitted in urgent thought. Helplessly tied and gagged as she was, how could she draw his attention?

The trail weaved, and Diana noticed a bright flash of light moving out on the prairie. As she continued staring in bewilderment, it slowly dawned on her that the light was caused by the sun's rays reflecting off her silver hatband. She confirmed the fact by wriggling her sharply drawn-back shoulders as much as she could, and the light bobbed up and down and from side to side with her movements.

Encouraged, Diana tried to keep her hat toward the sun as she rode along the serpentine path. She only hoped that the lone horseman would heed the reflection before Lonis discovered what was happening and put an end to the signal.

*

Matt Sutton drew in a quarter-mile from the foothills and sat studying the blinking light climbing up towards the mountains. The trail left by Diana and her captor led straight there, and chances were that, inadvertently or not, the light came from one of them. Since it wasn't stationary he gathered it was not the glint of a rifle that was waiting in ambush for him to come within range.

Diana's failed escape attempt had bought the needed time, forcing the outlaw to backtrack for miles to catch her, and then retrace his route. Confident that he would catch up with them and set things straight before the posse arrived, Matt put the paint forward.

Miles off, Andy Denham and his posse had come across the signs of Diana Logan's escape and recapture and a heated debate was in progress.

'It sure enough looks like the woman was trying to get away from the gent's company,' Amos Long stated.

'If so, then that means the outlaw has her and the tracks we think are his are really the other man's,' Jesse Seaton said thoughtfully.

'And ol' Wes done tangled with the wrong man,' Brick put in, relishing Wes's discomfort.

'We won't know for sure till we catch up with them,' Wes snapped, shooting Brick a look of pure poison.

'Whoever he is, he's still on their trail,' Andy said. 'And it's leading right to those mountains.'

'Let's stop wasting time and take advantage of

their delay,' Hiram Trask said authoritatively, 'before they become embedded in the mountains.'

Andy had no choice but to agree with the rancher and led the solemn group onward before the subject of the Utes could come up again. He would deal with that when and if they had to go into the mountains. He hoped to hell they wouldn't have to, as it sure wasn't a task he was looking forward to.

CHAPTER SIX

To Diana, the ride up the twisting mountain trail seemed endless. Her nerves worsened when it narrowed at times and her mare stumbled over ruts and stones. Tied helplessly in the saddle, a fatal stumble would send her with the horse into the rocky chasm below.

She was dully aware of the searing pains shooting up her spine into her sharply drawn back shoulders, which were already cramped from her bound arms. Despite her gloves her almost numb hands were cold as stones in a creek bottom. She bit down hard on her bulky gag, closed her eyes, and rode on, every nerve in her tall body crying out in agony with the continued jolting of her trotting horse, trying to divert her mind with comforting thoughts of the lone rider she'd seen and hopes of rescue.

Soon the trail grew better, but did little to relieve Diana's misery. She was pleased to see that the land on either side was broadening and realized they were moving further into the mountain, away from its edge. The thick piñons and cedars began giving way to taller timber, and she worried that the rider wouldn't be able to see the reflection from her hatband. The trail began to dip into a timbered canyon, and after a a few more agonizing miles they at last reached a wide clearing where they halted. Relieved, Diana sagged ungainly in the saddle.

Head raised, Lonis sat looking about and listening keenly. Shaded by the wide brim of his flat-crowned hat, his narrowed eyes swept the surrounding ridges as deep lines of tension carved his taut, stubbled face. Only the tang of pine and the scent of wood rotting in the damp earth reached his nostrils. The place seemed safe enough for now, and yet he couldn't relax completely. After all, a hunted man could never let down his guard. He heaved a weary sigh and dismounted, joints and muscles aching fiercely.

Turning to his captive he announced, 'As soon as I tend to you, I'm gonna have a better look around.'

Diana tensed inwardly but kept her suffering expression as she watched Lonis approach. She could only hope that he wouldn't spot the rider.

Alert, Matt Sutton proceeded up the switchback trail. With the thickening timber he had lost sight of the light, which he was pretty sure came from Diana's silver hatband. It didn't matter, as unencumbered by leading a horse as her captor was, he had closed the distance and should soon be upon them. He pulled the Winchester from its scabbard and levered a bullet into its chamber, the sound cracking loudly in the near-silence.

They had arrived too late.

The grim posse sat at the base of the foothills and let their exhausted horses blow. All eyes were on the trail winding up into the mountains that now took on an ominous appearance with the knowledge there was every chance they would encounter the Utes if they ventured into their territory after the outlaw and the man and woman.

'This is as far as I go,' Cal Burns, the livery stable-owner, said, breaking the tense quiet. 'I've got a wife and four kids to think about.' Several others chimed in, not all of them family men.

'All right,' Andy said wearily. 'Anyone who's going, do it now. There'll be no turning back once we get up there.'

'Snivelling cowards,' Elijah Hobson growled and made a gesture of disgust.

'It weren't my wife that was killed,' one of the saloon layabouts retorted.

'Dammit, don't hang around arguing,' Andy snapped. 'Git, and be done with it.'

The deserters needed no further urging. Almost in cavalry unison they wheeled their horses and put their spurs to them.

'We're now two men shy of a jury,' Brick Calloway observed drily, looking about at the nine other men.

'Three,' Andy corrected. 'A lawman can't serve on a jury.'

'Neither can a witness,' Orin Fowle stated.

'There's still enough of us to make it legal,' Hiram Trask said flatly.

'Yeah,' Wes seconded his father. 'And lawyer Seaton is still with us.'

'Suppose we worry about a trial when the time comes,' Seaton said softly.

'Won't need no trial if I git him in my gunsights,' Elijah Hobson said, and booted his horse up the narrow trail, leaving the others to follow strung out behind him.

Still gagged, Diana was kneeling uncomfortably against a pine. Her arms were stretched tautly above her head and secured slightly apart by ropes wound about the trunk. Other ropes circled her trim, corseted waist, and pinned each bare ankle to the sides of the bole. She had been made to strip to her brief black gambling costume before being tied in place, and her rigid position hitched her straining breasts almost over its low top. At least he hadn't left her there like that completely naked.

Disregarding the bark snagging loose strands of her long hair, Diana turned her head from side to side and saw that, except for her hobbled mare grazing nearby, she was still alone in the clearing. Though she had no liking for Lonis she wished he would return swiftly. The thought of a prowling bear or mountain cat, not to mention snakes and other crawlers, happening upon her was unnerving. She also wished that the rider (whom she hoped was Matt) or the posse would come and put an end to her captivity. Every second seemed an hour and every minute an eternity, as she waited, resigned, tensing at any sound, however slight.

By damn, he was right as rain!

Rafe Lonis's grimy face split into a wide, toothy grin, pleased that his instincts had been right. Being on the dodge had honed them to a fine point. Way back down the winding trail, weaving in and out of sight through the surrounding timber, was the single rider he thought he'd glimpsed some time ago. As he continued staring he recognized his old clothes and wondered in surprise how that fella had got a-hold of a horse and rifle.

Cussing fate, Lonis sat stewing and mentally sorting through his options. He really didn't want to kill the man or his horse. Besides, purposefully only winging a moving target weren't all that easy, particularly with him winding in and out of the trees. A missed shot would naturally lead to a shoot-out that would not only waste time, what with the posse somewheres behind, but might get him killed or bad hurt.

Lonis nodded thoughtfully. The girl was who the fella was after, and she was waiting there in the clearing, ready to lure him just like a bee to honey. Lonis could sure draw a steady bead when the man found her and was busying himself untying her. If it did lead to a killing so be it, but he wouldn't be the one dying. Rifle in hand, Lonis rose quietly and moved off to find his horse.

Nerves taut as bowstrings Matt continued his cautious ascent. Common sense told him not to push on too recklessly, as a bullet could be waiting behind any tree ahead. He would do himself and Diana no good if he got shot because of his own haste or carelessness. The posse (which he'd caught sight of several times before the trail had led away from the edge of the mountain) was too far behind to be a bother for the time being.

Keeping his mind solely on the business of tracking Diana and her captor, Matt rode on, rifle at the ready.

Scarcely giving his winded horse time to blow, Elijah Hobson set a gruelling pace and remained well ahead of the others. Andy Denham was content to allow Hobson to ride point. If the damn fool wanted to risk killing his horse or himself that was his own hard luck. Hobson could blunder upon some Utes just as easily as he could the outlaw.

Andy threw a look back at the eight men struggling along in single file. The trail was too narrow for much manoeuvring and they were sitting ducks if the outlaw or the Utes took a notion to make a fight. He turned and his sharp eyes ranged the path ahead in swift appraisal as they threaded their way higher and higher up the mountain in the vast sunlit stillness.

Damn it all, the sooner they were off this trail the better.

The girl was just as he'd left her. Her cheek was nestled against one upraised arm, long hair obscuring most of her gagged face, and she appeared to be sleeping. Her mare wandered about, grazing serenely in the wide clearing.

From his vantage point in the bushes directly across from Diana, Lonis had a clear shot whenever his pursuer arrived and went to free her. His ground-tied horse was back a-ways so as not to give away his hiding place. Lonis sighed impatiently; he hated this waiting game. The longer it took the *hombre* to show up the nearer the posse would be. He was sorely tempted to shoot off his rifle and hurry the fella along in the right direction but then thought better of it.

Time dragged by on leaden feet. Then Diana's horse suddenly raised its head and, ears pricked, nickered a greeting. Lonis caught the sound of hoofs approaching through the woods. He saw Diana stir, shake the hair from her eyes, and follow the mare's stare as she too heard the other horse pick its way through the trees. It wouldn't be long now. The muscles along Lonis's cheekbones quivered and jumped as he clenched and unclenched his jaws. In the stillness his breathing seemed to take on an added hoarseness. His finger gently tightened on the trigger.

A riderless horse appeared at one edge of the clearing, hesitated, then ambled toward the mare.

Cussing under his breath, eyes ablaze with excitement, Lonis's glance swept urgently about the trees and foliage surrounding the edge of the clearing. It was the fella's paint, all right – but where the hell had he got off to? Lonis tried to control his ragged breath as his heart and lungs did their damnedest to block his hearing. He'd hoped for a quick showdown. Instead, precious time would be squandered in a deadly game of cat-and-mouse. Refusing to panic and break cover, he lay belly-down, listening keenly for sounds of his elusive stalker.

The waiting was worse than before and wore on his already frayed nerves as he stared unblinkingly across the sunlit clearing, studying the area around the bound and gagged blonde kneeling rigidly against the tree. Lonis was aware of the sweat worming down his brow and cheeks, threatening his eyes with stinging salt, and restrained the urge to wipe it away. Any movement, however small, might reveal his position and invite a bullet.

Then something moved ever so slightly in the bushes to the right of the girl. It might be only the shadow from a breeze-blown bush – then again? Knowing he might not get another clear chance if it was indeed his pursuer, Lonis chanced squeezing off a round as the barely preceptible movement was repeated.

In unison with the shot came a hideous scream of mortal agony and a mad thrashing of bushes. The startled blonde jerked in her ropes and emitted a muffled scream that was quickly lost with the whin-nying of the frightened horses.

Urgently Lonis jacked another shell into the chamber and fired again at the swaying bushes. This time no sound came from there. Still, he threw several more bullets into that area as a precaution while the girl flinched and looked about wildly and the horses stamped and squealed. The diminishing gunshots chased one another higher into the surrounding mountains, then came only silence. Lonis waited prudently for a few more minutes before letting out an elated Rebel yell and shoving himself up.

He had almost gained his feet when an unyielding object caught him a glancing blow on the side of his head and hurled him face-down in the dirt, his brain exploding in a riot of sound and colour. While darkness engulfed him he did not lose consciousness, and had the presence of mind to realize that something had gone wrong. . . .

. . . awful wrong!

CHAPTER SEVEN

A harsh, indistinct voice was demanding something of him. Blinking away the darkness, Rafe Lonis rolled on his side and fumbled frantically for his Colt. As his fingers touched the butt, the toe of a boot smashed into his guts and hurled him over, flat on his back. His burning insides churned and he was momentarily paralysed. It was a gunfighter's trick. A man can take a blow or bullet about any place else and keep on shooting, but not in the guts. The shooter can them polish off his victim leisurely after he's helplessly inert and can't shoot back.

Through pain-blurred eyes Lonis saw the blonde's man drop his rifle, lean down and yank the six-gun from its holster. Then he gave in to the terrible pain and with a loud groan curled into a wretching ball. A boot to the kidneys straightened him out with a strangled yell and more agonized spasms. Keeping the Colt trained, Matt Sutton moved about and gathered both rifles under an arm while Lonis lay expressing his hurts with moans, groans, and shakes.

For long moments the two men regarded each other carefully. There was a cold and wicked anger in

57

Matt's grey eyes, and the muscles along his strong jawline stood out. It was obvious he was exerting all of his will-power to keep from pulling the trigger. Lonis mentally cussed himself with blistering venom at being taken in by such an old trick as a feigned dying scream in the bushes.

'All right,' Matt said tightly, 'let's go free Diana and then see just exactly who it was you shot.'

Lonis's face plainly showed his surprise. 'I done thought it 'twas you.'

'You thought wrong. Now get up from there nice 'n easy.'

Making it appear more of a chore than it was, Lonis groaned and shoved himself up slowly on all fours, hands braced against the leaf and pine-needle covered ground. Weighing his chances, he curled his fingers into the dirt, only to have Matt thumb back the Colt's hammer. 'Don't even think about it,' he cautioned sternly. 'Now quit stalling.' Lonis wisely obeyed and, gaining his unsteady feet, led the way out into the clearing.

Diana gasped for breath around her gag as she elatedly recognized Matt cautiously trailing Lonis toward her. Tears welled in her eyes and it was all she could do to keep from sobbing in relief. Somebody had been shot in the nearby bushes, and thank heavens it hadn't been Matt. Batting drops from her long sable lashes, she watched them pass the two horses and come to a halt before her.

'Get that cloth outta her mouth first,' Matt said, hard, 'then untie her.'

Lonis crouched stiffly to one side of Diana, who sat

58

there staring up in disbelief at Matt, then turned away and lowered her head so he could reach the tight knot at the nape of her neck. His fingers picked and plucked awkwardly at the twist of cloth, painfully pulling strands of her hair that were caught in it. Suddenly one of the horses blew loudly, showing alarm, and he paused in his work.

Distant hoofbeats were racing across the ground, a crowd of them pounding toward the clearing. It was the posse, drawn by the earlier wild gunshots.

For a brief moment all three were listening and looking off tensely in that direction, and Lonis took a desperate chance by hurling himself sideways into Matt's legs. Rifles dropping from under his arm, Colt aborting and deafening them with its booming report, Matt was slammed to the ground by the savage weight of Lonis's body.

Eyes saucers above her still-tight gag, Diana knelt staring fearfully as Lonis snaked his way up Matt's long body, clawing for the gun. Trembling muscles standing out in clear profile, she disregarded the various hurts to her lithe body and strained uselessly at her taut ropes while the men flailed about in a twisting, tumbling heap of furiously wriggling arms and legs.

The gun fell from Matt's hand and Lonis moved up on him, grabbing for it. Matt swung his fists wildly. A blow crashed into the outlaw's face and the madly clutching hands abruptly released him. Matt threw him off with a powerful head-butt to the belly and Lonis rolled away. Matt made a leap and was astride Lonis, pinning him down. He again began slugging wildly, lost in his anger. Then Lonis bucked him off, and clung to him as they both rose and were finally erect, facing each other.

The men closed, clenched fists smashing at each other, trying to finish the fight with deadly, mauling blows. Matt couldn't remember the number of blows he took or gave before Lonis began to weaken under the wild, sledge-hammer pounding of his fists. Eyes flaming, Matt moved in closer and drove his fist savagely at Lonis's head. The blow connected solidly and spun the outlaw toward the edge of the clearing.

Following, Matt stepped in and hit left and right to Lonis's head, very hard, stepped out again, waited for him to lunge, then got in two more to the head. Lonis rebounded off a tree, and he and Matt charged each other, fists flying. Matt ducked a flailing left, caught a glancing right to the jaw that shook him to his boot heels, then covered his head with his arms as Lonis came charging in.

Suddenly Matt's right arm swung in a short, vicious arc. Bone crunched against bone and the outlaw reeled drunkenly into the tree. Matt was on him, pumping both fists at his belly. Then he switched his attack solely to the head and his crashing fists tore into Lonis's jaw. The outlaw would have fallen except that Matt's continuing punches kept him nailed to the tree.

Finally Lonis started a limp, downward slide, but Matt grabbed his shirt front and hauled him up again. Bracing Lonis against the trunk, Matt released him, drew back a fist and swung. Lonis sprawled over sideways under the force of a last savage hook and lay bloody, beaten and unconscious. Sucking in mighty gulps of air, Matt stood swaying over his foe, weary arms dangling loosely at his sides.

Slowly, the growing thunder of the nearing posse cut through Matt's ebbing rage and fatigue. He turned hastily to Diana, watching him with large, relieved eyes, then abruptly remembered the gunshot victim. Was he a posse member? Matt knew he'd better find out – and fast. Calling to Diana that he'd be with her directly, Matt shoved into the thick bushes.

It took only seconds to locate the body, and things were far worse than Matt had feared. He had never seen a Ute before, but Matt was sure he was looking at one now. The brave was no more than late teens, and his bare, bronzed torso was peppered with ugly, bloody holes from Lonis's rifle. His face, frozen in a death-grimace, was devoid of warpaint, and the heads of the arrows in his quiver were for hunting not fighting. Just as bad, another set of moccasin tracks led stumbling away along with a trail of blood.

Matt broke into a run and followed the footprints to an open patch of ground where two unshod ponies had stood. The wounded brave had ridden off leading the other pony, and more than likely a war party would soon come for both the body and revenge. He had to get Diana off this mountain before that happened. Aware of the posse bearing down, Matt whirled and raced back to the clearing.

Diana's face brightened as Matt burst from the bushes and, ignoring Lonis's unconscious heap, ran to her. As he dropped to a knee and tugged at her gag, horsemen charged into the clearing from all directions, guns drawn. A man with a star on his chest shouted for him to get away from her and raise his hands.

'Or we'll gladly fill yuh so full o' holes you won't float in brine!' Brick Calloway added, caught up in the moment of capture.

'That's the fella,' Wes Trask stated, 'and there's my horse!' He hastily jerked a thumb toward the nervous paint standing with the mare on one side of the clearing. 'Horse stealing alone is a crime. Let's string him up and be done with it!' Excited by the chase the other ranch hands and remaining saloon toughs piped in eagerly with him.

'So is shooting an innocent, unarmed man without warning!' Matt said flatly, meeting Wes's eyes accusingly. His words confirmed Andy Denham and several others' suspicions about what had really happened during that encounter. Matt shifted his gaze to Andy. 'The man you're after, Deputy, is over there.' He nodded toward Lonis who was showing feeble signs of regaining consciousness.

'You're wearin' the clothes of the man we want,' Elijah Hobson snarled. 'Ain't that right, Fowle?'

'Sure 'nuff is,' Orin Fowle agreed without hesitation.

'It wasn't my idea,' Matt said. 'He switched with me.' Seeing the sceptical faces, he looked down at Diana. 'My girl can tell you, if you'll let me get her loose.'

Aware that all eyes were on her, Diana nodded and made muffled sounds of agreement. Her tongue prodded the loosened ball of cloth between her teeth. Reluctantly it came free, rolled down her chin, and fell about her neck. She sighed and started to speak but Wes Trask interrupted.

'Who's gonna take the word of a saloon trollop!'

'Shut your dirty mouth, boy,' Matt bristled, 'or, guns or no guns, I'll knock you off your horse again and pound some manners into you.' Wes flushed and shifted sheepishly in the saddle, purposely averting his eyes from his father and the cowhands. 'Diana is a lady and a gambler by profession,' Matt said pointedly. Still, many faces in the group remained dubious.

'The lady has no reason to lie,' Jesse Seaton said quietly, acting the voice of reason. 'Suppose we hear her out.'

'That's right,' Andy put in forcefully, still trying to keep his authority. 'Now settle down and listen.'

Diana had often been the centre of attention, but now instead of admiration the sombre faces around her told clearly that it was a crucial matter of life and death. She spoke with difficulty; it had been so long since she had used her voice that it sounded rusty and harsh. She felt a small embarrassment, fearing it might confirm the belief that she was a harlot. Diana pressed on, keeping the story terse and precise. By the time she had finished there was no longer any lingering doubt as to Matt's innocence.

Andy exchanged a nod of agreement with Seaton, then addressed Matt. 'Go ahead and free the lady, then you two can be on your way.'

While Matt knelt and went to work on Diana's

ropes, the posse's attention shifted over to Rafe Lonis, who was now sitting up groggily on an elbow. Again trying to run things, Hiram Trask said soberly, 'Fowle, tell our judge, lawyer Seaton, and the rest of us jury members just what you saw so we can make this hanging legal.'

'Whoa, now,' Lonis protested, his face paling behind its stubble, 'I never laid a finger on her – and that's the God's honest truth!' He was shouted down, and several cowhands hustled him, yelling, fighting and kicking, to a big pine with a sturdy limb on the other side of the clearing. Then Fowle began relating what he'd seen that day to the self-appointed judge and jury.

'I don't like him any more than you do,' Diana said, rubbing her wrists and wincing at the fiery pinpricks that came with the sluggish return of her circulation, 'but, Matt, I believe he's innocent.' Matt pulled the rope from about her waist and stared at her incredulously. 'Except to tie and gag me,' she explained, 'he never tried to touch me – and he certainly had many chances to do so.'

'Maybe he just didn't have the hankering,' Matt said, and then started on the ropes around one of her tapered ankles. 'Being chased sorta takes away a man's appetite for food and "other" things.'

'But if he is innocent,' Diana persisted, 'then a killer will go free.' Matt made no reply and moved around the tree to untie her other ankle. Before Diana could continue an uproar from across the clearing announced that Lonis had been found guilty. Discarding the last ropes, Matt helped Diana to her bare feet and held her arm while she leaned against the tree until she regained the use of her cramped, long, lovely legs. Then Andy Denham's desperate, shouting voice drew their attention back to the posse.

'This ain't legal, and you all know it. He's going back to town with us and wait for the circuit judge.'

'Says you,' Elijah Hobson challenged. 'He'll hang anyways, so do it here and now!'

As others shouted in agreement, Andy threw a desperate look about for support and was dejected to see there was none. Storekeeper Amos Long was hanging back timidly at the edge of the group while Seaton, evidently satisfied with his sentence, sat watching placidly with what appeared to be a half-smile on his face. The few others he had counted on to side him had either left the posse or were part of the mob.

A rope was tossed over the high branch. Its noosed end was pulled down to slip over Lonis's neck while he was held by a multitude of hands and his wrists were tied behind him. He struggled madly and insisted sobbingly that he was innocent. His words went unheeded and a horse was led to him.

'All right, that's enough!' Andy shouted over the din and reached for his pistol. Wes pushed his horse up and, with a seemingly casual movement, rose in his stirrups and slammed his Colt down on top of the deputy's head. The crushed hat crown gave scant protection, and Andy slouched from the saddle, stunned.

'Matt . . .' Diana implored, her slender fingers

digging into his arm.

'Guilty or not,' Matt relented, 'he's not hanging in my clothes.' Giving a tight, reassuring smile, he left Diana, still weak-kneed and clinging to the tree, and rushed to his guns that had gone unnoticed in the thick grass by the posse. A pistol shot parted the rope on the branch and startled the group before Lonis's resisting form could be put on the horse. All eyes turned to Matt.

'Are you mixing in this, stranger?' Hiram Trask snarled, his voice as ugly as his distorted face.

'I'm trying to save your lives,' Matt replied and motioned to some nearby bushes. 'Take a look behind there and you'll find a dead Indian, shot by that fella. Tracks show a wounded second one got away. It happened by accident during all that shooting, which he thought was at me. Reckon there'll be a war party showing up about any time now.'

'That's all the more reason to hang this here killer,' Hiram Trask insisted.

'If you're smart you'll put him on a horse and take him along like the deputy wants, instead of dilly-dallying around for a lynching.'

'Matt, look,' Diana called urgently, pointing up at the shadows between the trees and rocks on the ridge above.

Matt followed her gaze and froze abruptly, an icy chill rippling through him. Past the boulders, high up on the ridge, a mounted Ute warrior sat his pony watching them. A second mounted figure appeared and halted beside him. Then a third brave rode up behind the first two and was followed by a fourth. All had rifles, and they were staring and gesturing down at the group in the clearing. Sure as taxes there were more painted warriors up there somewhere.

Time had run out. The only thing to do now was skedaddle – and fast!

CHAPTER EIGHT

Signal smoke rose high into the cloudless afternoon sky from beyond a distant ridge as the posse descended a serpentine mountain trail with as much haste as was dared. Instead of a helter-skelter flight, the group had quit the clearing in an orderly manner befitting a cavalry manoeuvre. The appearance of the Ute band had brought a sobering of emotions and all thoughts of a hanging had vanished for the present. Rafe Lonis had been tied on the pack horse, and Wes Trask and Brick Calloway had reclaimed their own mounts, as had Matt Sutton, though he still wore the outlaw's clothes. Diana Logan had slipped her riding clothes over her gambling outfit and was following behind Matt.

Since there was relative safety in numbers, the two were forced to join with the posse until the threat of danger was past; even if it meant riding all the way to the town of Willow Creek. There had been detours before, and while it was a necessary annoyance, Diana hoped their presence as strangers would have a restraining effect on the hot-heads in the posse. Diana held to her belief in Lonis's innocence and, though she and Matt weren't Pinkerton detectives, she felt they might help ferret out the real killer – providing he was among the men.

Matt Sutton had no liking for the men or Rafe Lonis, and as soon as it was safe he and Diana would take their leave of the posse. The deputy seemed weak and unsure of himself, and Matt wouldn't take any bets that Lonis would complete the ride back to Willow Creek, once he and Diana pulled out. But right now the only concern was getting off the mountain and away from the Utes.

Andy Denham was in a sour mood. His head throbbed with every step of his jogging horse, and he vowed to pay Wes Trask back in spades for the clout on his head. Merely reporting Wes's action to Sheriff Crandall would only mean a reprimand for the little bastard, as the older lawman was beholden to Hiram Trask for his job and usually tried to keep in his good graces. Still, Andy would somehow get back at Wes, no matter how long it took.

Amos Long had proved to be a disappointment. He had hung back in silence, fence-straddling because of his store and the fear of a boycott by Hiram Trask, whose ranch's patronage was a major source of income. Another disappointment had been Jesse Seaton's participation in the near-hanging. Andy had counted on the lawyer to stand with him against the hot-heads. When it came to a showdown a body sure found out fast who his friends were, and amongst this lot there was none.

Despite their run-in with him, the stranger and his woman seemed interested in the outlaw getting a fair trial. Even so, Andy felt sure the verdict would still be the same. But he did hope the couple would stick with the posse all the way to town, just in case this bunch got lynch-happy again once they were clear of the Utes.

Rafe Lonis was in the depths of despair. Once more fate had dealt him a card from the bottom of the deck. Of course he had to admit reluctantly that it had been partly his own fault. This morning he'd been free and clear, with a horse, different set of clothes, money and grub, and a chance to get clean away. What on earth had possessed him to take the girl with him? She had slowed him down from the first, and her near-escape later had been his undoing. He should have let her go. The time wasted gave her man a chance to gain on them, not to mention the damn posse. Even then, maybe if he'd just left her tied in the clearing her man might have been satisfied to get her back. Lonis had then wasted more time setting an ambush that didn't work. Thank God it hadn't, or he would have been strung up by the posse.

Trying to content himself that at least one thing had worked out right for him, Lonis thought about the long ride back to Willow Creek. If they dodged the Indians and Diana and her man stayed with the posse, then he should complete the journey safely. All wasn't totally lost, as during a trek there would come a time when somebody got a little careless. When that time did come he had to be ready to take advantage, even if he was still tied on the pack horse – and he might not be when and if something happened. He tried to ignore the various aches from both his beating and the tight ropes on his wrists and booted ankles and stay vigilant, without appearing to be.

Wes Trask was also nursing a grudge. The stranger had made him look a fool in front of his father and the whole posse. Before they parted company Wes was going to put him in his place and redeem his lost prestige. Though he'd never been in a real gunfight, Wes had backed down more than a few *hombres* with his fast draw. He was confident he could do the same with the stranger, and the way to go about it was through his girl. It would be an even greater pleasure to shame him in front of her. Whore or lady gambler, she was a looker, and Wes would surely like to enjoy himself with her for a spell.

Casting occasional backward glances, the posse rode on in silence, each lost in his own grim thoughts. The talking smoke continued to rise into the sky but the Utes remained out of sight. The question was how much longer would they do so?

It was late afternoon when the posse came off the mountain into the foothills, and the Utes finally made their presence known. A party of thirty warriors broke from behind two hills ahead and blocked the way. Faces streaked with warpaint, rifles resting athwart their saddles, they sat staring in silence. Other bands crested the tops of the two hills, and a look back up the trail revealed a winding line that took the shape of men and horses.

'They got us trapped!' cried one of the cowhands.

'Not by a long shot!' Hiram Trask shouted and, with a savage wrench on his reins, dug his heels into the flanks of his horse and led the unhesitating group along the foot of the mountain. Howling and firing, the Utes came pouring down off the hills and gave chase.

Besides searching for a protected place to make a stand, the group watched the ground ahead of their horses for any holes the animals might step in. None wanted to be toppled to the earth for the Utes to ride down. The Utes were several hundred yards away and didn't seem to be gaining. The firing was relatively harmless, as it was nigh impossible for a galloping horseman to hit another, especially while racing over rough, uneven ground. Still, on they came, kicking up billowing clouds of dust and shrieking and firing.

Suddenly another group was seen riding up from a wash and paralleling them. It was evident the Utes knew another, faster way off the mountain than the trail the posse had taken. The band began angling in, and the men knew they had to find cover before they were cut off and trapped.

Then they came upon the right spot.

A large group of rocks lay clustered about before the mountain, whose rocky overhang prevented the Utes from sneaking behind them and shooting down from above. A desperate spurt of speed put the possemen to the rocks well ahead of their pursuers. The men leaped from their saddles, jerked their rifles from scabbards, and hastily fanned out, taking positions behind the rocks. Armed with Matt's pistol, Diana was stationed out of harm's way behind several boulders to guard Rafe Lonis, who was bound hand and foot, and the group's horses.

Most were experienced Indian fighters and had served one side or the other during the War Between the States and knew to keep a cool head and conserve bullets. A former colonel in the Union militia, Hiram Trask stressed firing discipline. Their shots should be spaced so their weapons weren't emptied at the same time, and there was a continuous wall of fire that would break any attack.

The tense quiet exploded in a racket of yelling, firing and drumming hoofs as the Utes came charging across the flat, open ground. It was the sort of foolishness that the defenders had counted on, the wild, unreasoning charge that nearly always made the Indian a sitting duck. Breaths held in an agony of suspense, the group waited, resisting the urge to shoot as soon and as fast as possible. It would be sheer folly, comparable to the Utes' error in trying to ride down their foe. Although the wait seemed endless, it was only a matter of seconds before the lead rank was within range. Still, they were allowed to come ahead until at almost point-blank range there was a deafening crash of rifles.

The crushing volley slammed into the charging Utes and the lead warriors went down in a mad tangle of screaming, wounded and dying men and horses. Firing coolly, the posse showered hot lead into the hollering mass as the following ranks stacked up, the force of their charge broken by the dead and dying braves and horses writhing before them. Several shots were hurled after the retreating Utes, who rode to join up with the other approaching bands.

A harsh silence slowly settled in. How long it would last was anybody's guess. All knew the Utes would be back to hit them again and again, until the defenders were dead or it was decided the attackers had suffered enough losses and it was deemed fruitless to continue any longer. The wind fluttered their clothing and that of the dead Utes and their horses' manes, bringing the stench of death wafting across to rock fortress. Several long hours of daylight lay ahead before the respite of night, and many wondered if they would last until then. Either way the group was determined not to sell their lives cheaply.

The buzzing of flies sounded like a nest of angry hornets as they swooped down in a black mass upon the pile of dead men and animals. The defenders watched, waited, drank sparingly from their canteens and picked bullets from their cartridge belts and shoved them into their weapons' loading gates. Every man wanted a full rifle and pistol when the next attack came.

And they did not have long to wait.

CHAPTER NINE

Body rigid to keep what he was doing from being given away by any movement, Rafe Lonis sat against a boulder, sawing his wrist ropes against a ridge of rock his fingers had unearthed in the dirt before the first Ute attack. He worked in the grip of remorseless tension as Diana's large eyes darted nervously from him to the hobbled horses and back again while wincing at the loud, violent sounds of the battle being waged on the other side of the shielding boulders. Besides the hope of escaping during the battle, Lonis hated the thought of being found helpless, should the Utes overrun the posse. He doubted the girl would have the chance, much less the gumption, to shoot him dead first. Indians made torture last for hours – even a short time could seem an eternity – and that terrified him much more than hanging.

As the war cries, men's cussing, horses' hoofbeats, and dying screams merged with the rapid firing, Diana's wide-eyed attention once more went to the side of the nearest boulder, away from Lonis – and at that moment the last strand of the rope's fibre finally parted. Disregarding the tingling pains shooting through his wrists and arms as his blood began to course unhampered once again, Lonis lunged desperately at the distracted blonde sitting across from him.

Caught by surprise, Diana was hurled to the ground hard as Lonis smashed into her heavily. The six-gun discharged into the boulder, chipping rock and debris, and flew from her jostled hand. The shot went unnoticed, as did her small, startled cry that was cut short by the breath being driven from her body and the back of her head slamming against the firm earth. Then Lonis's fist clipped her on the point of her chin and everything went black.

Snatching the pistol in his awkward, near-numb hand, Lonis shoved himself to his knees and threw a hasty glance at the side of the boulder. As he'd hoped, no one was coming to investigate the shot. He set the gun beside him and clawed at the knotted rope about his ankles. His punch hadn't had his full strength behind it, and the blonde moaned and stirred weakly, showing signs that she would be coming around soon. Lonis jerked the rope free and grabbed the gun. He raised it for a blow but hesitated, mentally debating in spite of his predicament.

His movements were still uncoordinated and there was the fear of accidentally striking her too hard. Such a blow could kill, or badly damage her skull. Like he'd said before, he was a lot of things but he wasn't a murderer – especially of helpless women.

Reminding himself that at the moment all the men were hidden in the rocks busily fighting for their lives and no one cared a damn about him as

long as the attack kept up, Lonis sighed disgustedly
and lowered his menacing arm. Cussing himself for a
soft-hearted fool, he stuffed the Colt into his belt,
rolled Diana's slack body over on her stomach, and
began looping the rope tightly about her crossed
wrists.

The battle continued to rage furiously as the Utes,
crouched low on their ponies, came in repeatedly
wave after shooting and screaming wave. There was
firing all around Matt, who waited until his targets
were close at hand before he opened up with his
Winchester, working the lever and squeezing the trigger in a single, smooth motion.

A few feet away, Elijah Hobson knelt beside a rock,
hunched over to make his large, partly exposed bulk
as small a target as possible, firing his Henry fifteen-
shot repeating rifle slowly and carefully at the
oncoming braves.

Nearby a saloon tough dropped his rifle as bullets
whined and slapped the air overhead, some ricocheting off rocks, and sprawled on his face in the
dirt, blood leaking into a widening puddle from a
hole in his temple.

Yards away, Jesse Seaton left his rock and ran,
crouched, for a small boulder down at the end of the
line, alternately firing the six-guns in each hand as he
went. To any who spared a thought, it merely
appeared he wanted better shelter, but Seaton had
secret business with Orin Fowle who was covering
their far right flank by himself. Seaton had emptied
his weapons by the time he got there and, panting,

slipped down behind the small boulder, out of sight from the others.

Fowle spared him a half-questioning glance but appeared glad to have company for once. Neither spoke. The Utes were closer, galloping straight at them. Seaton fumbled bullets urgently from the row of loops on his shell belt. Fowle's rapidly firing Winchester kept the howling pack at bay until Seaton was able to reload and join in the carnage.

Rafe Lonis knotted the scarf's ends firmly at the back of Diana's head, drawing the thinly folded strip of cloth past her lips and teeth and muffling her soft moans. He'd finished his task in the nick of time, as consciousness was beginning a slow return. Quickly, he surveyed the ropes holding the girl in a strict, back-arching hog-tie. Then, satisfied that she would remain there helpless until somebody found her (he sure hoped it wasn't the Utes), he shoved to his feet and strode to the horses.

Selecting Hiram Trask's black gelding, Lonis removed the hobbles and led the animal off into the rocks as the firing became sporadic. He hoped to hell the Utes would keep up the attack until he was in a safe position for a getaway. Also, that way nobody would go checking on the girl any time soon and find her prisoner had escaped. He led the black on, then halted abruptly as the sound of nearby voices came to him from beyond the boulder in a momentary pause in the firing on the far right flank. Breath caught in his chest, Lonis covered the horse's muzzle against any sudden whinny and peered cautiously around the side of the rock, to see Orin Fowle and Jesse Seaton in a heated conversation only yards away.

'You tryin' to go back on our agreement to make me a rich man?' Fowle demanded, his face set in a scowl of growing rage.

'I didn't take you to raise for life,' Seaton said coldly. 'A one-time payment of a thousand dollars to keep your mouth shut is more than fair.'

'That was before I had to lie an innocent man into a hangman's noose. I got a delicate conscience.'

'It didn't appear to bother you back up on the mountain before that cowboy broke up the hanging.'

'Well, it does now – and I'm gonna hafta do it again when we get that jasper back to town for trial. It was a heap different when we thought he was gonna give us the slip.'

They studied each other for a long moment, then Seaton relented reluctantly. 'All right. Two thousand – and that is final.'

A cunning smile spread over Fowle's stubbled face and he pressed his advantage. 'Let's us just say twenty-five hundred a year. That rich, *homely* wife of yours ain't gonna miss it. You made a few bad investments and had some gambling losses.'

'The hell you say!'

'That ain't much to keep your neck out of a noose.'

'You keep on, Fowle, and your greed will do you out of anything.'

'I don't think so, *Mister Lawyer*. I'm holdin' all the cards in this hand.'

'Frankly, it's your word against mine. Who the hell

do you think people will believe? I have no reason to have murdered Ellen Hobson.'

'I can think of a real good 'un. I been seein' you come an' go from Hobson's place when he ain't there for over a year. Might just be that *little bundle* Miz Hobson were expectin' didn't belong to her husband at all.' He was rewarded as a slight flicker of apprehension flittered across Seaton's handsome face. 'That's it, ain't it? She wanted you to leave your wife and her money and go off with her and your baby.' He grinned widely and shook his head. 'That sure weren't the fatherly thing to do, now was it?'

Seaton didn't share the humour and was grimly silent, mentally cursing himself for underestimating Fowle. Still, that was an error easily rectified. Before he could respond a horse's impatient nicker and stamping of hoofs whirled him around. Fowle followed his movement.

The sweeping red rage that Rafe Lonis felt on learning the two were not only responsible for his near-death and, if they got out of this fix, his certain hanging when the posse reached town and a speedy trial was held, caused him to forget about keeping his horse silent. The fat was in the fire now, and there was only one thing to do. Raising his pistol he stepped out from the side of the boulder. Luck was with him. The men were utterly stunned by the very unexpected sight of him.

'Awright, you bastards,' Lonis growled, 'we're gonna find that deputy so's you can square things for me!'

The two were just recovering from their surprise

and it appeared that Lonis had the drop on them. But a sudden rifle shot from a charging Ute missed Lonis by scant inches and hurled dust and rock splinters into the side of his face, stinging and momentarily blinding him. The yipping buck bore down, levelling shells into his old Henry repeater. The shots ricocheted off the boulder, missing Lonis as he staggered about cussing and knuckling his eyes.

All in one long, swift, fluid movement Seaton brought his six-guns up and simultaneously shot Lonis, ahead of him, and Fowle, on his left, in their chests, then spun and fired at the fast-approaching Ute and a second brave behind him, silencing their war cries and flinging them from their mounts.

Pistol bucking from his hand as it discharged harmlessly into the ground, spewing up dirt, Lonis wilted down the side of the boulder, leaving a red streak to mark the path of his descent. He sat heavily with a thump, arms limp at his sides, legs spraddled, and chin resting on his chest.

Seaton turned his attention back to those near him. Fowle lay on his back staring unblinkingly at the sun with wide eyes full of pain and surprise, his mouth open in silent protest, a grimace distorting his features. Yards away, Lonis sat unmoving against the boulder, and to any who came upon the scene it would appear that he and Fowle had killed each other. No Utes were charging his position, so Seaton stood and, crouching low, made his way back toward the others who were busily engaged in beating back a fresh attack.

*

Groggy and confused, Diana Logan awoke slowly to the nightmarish sounds of rapid gunfire, men's excited, cursing voices, and death screams of men and horses mixing with savage war cries. An effort to cover her ears and shut out the clamour brought instant tugging pains to her crossed wrists and booted ankles, causing her to bite down hard on the tight cloth that muted her gasping moans. The act also bothered her aching jaw, which added to her misery. She lay still, letting her aches slowly fade while her hazy mind composed itself, and realized that through her own negligence she was once again in Rafe Lonis's tight ropes.

Diana looked toward the horses and noticed that the solid black one belonging to the bossy old rancher was gone. She was pleased. It couldn't have happened to a more deserving person, except perhaps his son. Anyway, Lonis was an excellent judge of horses. If he did manage to slip away from here unseen, he stood a very good chance of outrunning the Utes. She couldn't fault him for trying; to stay meant death by hanging, unless the real killer was unmasked.

The sounds of violence diminished as both sides settled down to sniping. She was certainly safe enough back here on the ground. Summoning her strength, Diana made an attempt to free herself. In only a minute or so she knew painfully that she was accomplishing nothing but self-inflicted harm to her still rope-sore wrists and ankles, though the leather boots did offer some protection. Lonis's knots were as inescapable as ever, and all she could do was lie there helplessly until Matt or one of the men came to check on her and the prisoner. Seeking to maintain the feeling in her limbs for as long as possible, she went limp in her ropes. It might be some time before anyone found her.

Minutes dragged by like hours, punctuated occasionally by gunshots, then Diana heard heavy footsteps approaching and raised her cheek from the ground. She knew all but Matt would blame her, and rightfully so. But would they accuse her of purposely letting Lonis escape? And if so, would they believe her denial? Nerves and body taut, she turned her head in that direction and waited tensely.

CHAPTER TEN

Elijah Hobson could not wait a second longer. Everybody was busy trying to pick off an Indian so the time was just right. The girl would give him no trouble. He could disarm her easy enough, then put a fatal bullet in the drifter before she could even scream for help. Hell, it wasn't really cold-blooded murder. The man had a fair trial with a judge and jury, and had been found guilty as sin. This would be an execution, plain and simple. Only instead of hanging, he would be shot dead. Maybe that was a mite too quick, but justice would still be done.

Hobson rounded the side of the boulder and halted, dead-still, clutching his rifle, surprise on his grim face. The girl lay there hog-tied with the man's ropes and gagged with her own scarf, and there was no sign of the prisoner. His eyes swept to the horses. Hiram Trask's black gelding was gone. He had been cheated. Justice still had a long way to go before being done.

'Damn you to eternal hell for this, woman,' Hobson managed between clenched teeth. 'I oughta kill the both of you!' Leaving Diana feeling the intensity of his rage, he charged off.

Through a golden spider web of her long, tousled hair Diana watched Hobson clamber into the rocks, following the tracks. She hoped Rafe Lonis had made his escape, for Hobson had every intention of killing him. She looked about frantically but she was alone again. Then she gave a start as a voice cried, 'Look, they're gathering for another attack!'

In the rocks, Matt levered a shell into his Winchester's chamber and glanced over at Andy Denham nearby. 'The chief is arguing for at least one more attack.' He pointed toward the warbonneted man riding back and forth and waving a lance decorated with scalps while addressing the line of horsemen. 'He'll be with them this time, to show how powerful his medicine is. Aim for him and nobody else. Pass it on to the others. We get him, and that'll be it until they can choose a new chief with stronger medicine. And that most likely won't be any time soon.'

While word was being passed around the men checked their weapons and watched the chief whip the warriors into a screaming frenzy. And then the line broke, with the chief in the lead, and they came thundering toward the rocks, shouting and firing.

Haste nullifying stealth, Elijah Hobson blundered through the rocks. The drumming of hoofs and bloodthirsty screams jerked his attention from the tracks he was following, and he looked out on the broad expanse. The colourful array of feathers, warpaint, horses, and gleaming ornaments and weapons inspired no awe and brought only a curse, as he felt forced to stop his hunt and rejoin the fight. Resting his rifle on top of a rock, he watched impatiently while the shouting horde drew closer without the defenders firing a shot.

'C'mon, shoot, damn you,' he muttered and drew a bead on the chief, who was several yards ahead of the racing warriors.

Before Hobson could pull the trigger the defenders unleashed a volley in unison. The chief lunged high on his mount, shaking wildly, his scalp-hung lance shattering, and seemed to dance in the air as his horse went down head over heels. It was as though the man had run smack into an invisible wall. The warriors jerked in their horses and stared in silence at their fallen chief. Then they began a lament and two warriors walked their horses forward to collect the dead man. That was when Hobson opened up with his Henry, sending both braves spinning from their mounts, dead before they hit the ground.

'Hold it,' Andy Denham shouted. 'Let them fetch their dead!'

Regardless, Hobson planned on knocking down two more but the sudden close-by whinny of a horse stopped him. Whirling, he ran on in the direction of the tracks, and, rounding a boulder, came upon Hiram Trask's black horse. The animal shied and nickered as he approached, rifle ready. He spoke low and soothingly while edging around the horse and the side of a boulder. Once more Hobson was halted by an unexpected scene before him.

The killer sat propped against the boulder, a bloody hole in his chest and a gun near his right hand. Yards ahead, Orin Fowle lay sprawled on his back. It appeared the men had shot each other.

Kicking the pistol further away from the killer's hand in the unlikely event that he wasn't dead and would make a grab for it, Hobson moved forward for a closer look at Fowle. There was no doubt he was dead, shot through the middle of his chest. Hobson became aware that he was standing, making a perfect target above the cluster of rocks. He started to crouch but saw the Utes, their lament building, riding slowly away, their chief's body supported between two horsemen. He smiled in satisfaction at the sight of the two warriors that he'd killed slung across their horses' backs. Common sense told him to let well enough alone. Any more shooting and the braves might become so riled they would forget about delaying while choosing a new chief and commence warring again.

Matt and the rest watched the Utes depart, and more than one man drew a long sigh of relief. A quick check showed only one man dead and a few with minor wounds. Then they heard Hobson's excited call.

'Hey, everybody, come a-running!'

Exchanging confused glances, the group rushed off through the rocks. They emerged, with Andy and Matt in the lead, and saw Hobson waiting in a small clearing with two downed men. Bringing up the rear,

Wes Trask took a quick look at the scene before them, then whirled and ran back for the clearing where Diana and the horses were waiting.

'Fowle done the deed for us,' Hobson remarked, and motioned about at the bodies.

'How in hell did he git there?' Brick Calloway asked, staring at Rafe Lonis.

'That's my horse,' Hiram Trask exclaimed, spotting the black, reins dragging the ground, standing by the boulder, well away from the smell of Lonis's blood.

Concern for Diana spun Matt around and sent him bolting away without waiting while the bodies were checked.

Diana heard running footsteps and managed to roll laboriously on to her side and turn at the waist, facing in that direction. Judging that the battle was finally over, her face brightened at the prospect of Matt coming to see how she was faring. On seeing Wes Trask round the boulder, her expression immediately became a frown.

Wes halted, his eyes inching over Diana's cramped form, taking in her tautly jutting breasts and utter helplessness.

'Well now, I do declare,' he said, voice smart and sassy, 'what have we here?' He moved to her. 'Did that mean killer jump you and do that?' He stopped and stood over her. 'Or is it just to hide you letting him go?' He smiled, amused, as Diana's features became as cold as a blue norther. Then his smile turned ugly. 'You know what happens to pretty young *ladies* who lie?' He dropped to his knees and raised her torso by her sharply pulled back shoulders. 'They get kissed . . . for starters.' He lowered his face and slammed his mouth against her lips, protruding above and below her tight gag, crushing them agonizingly against her teeth. Diana emitted muffled protests of pain and rage as she writhed in his grip, shaking her head in an attempt to break the kiss. Then they became aware of rushing footsteps.

'Get the hell away from her, you little bastard!' Matt shouted, hard.

Wes turned his head toward Matt but retained his grip on Diana's slim shoulders. 'I ain't hurting her any, cowboy,' he growled. 'Just go away, and you can have her back in a bit – good as new.' His laugh was mean and taunting.

Matt took a step forward and squared himself; get too close to a man in a gunfight and there's a good likelihood he can also nail you while he's going down. 'When you get up from there, you can either draw or use your fists. Makes no nevermind to me, except the first way is permanent.'

Wes shoved Diana's torso to the ground, smashing her tied arms beneath her bent body and bringing an involuntary muffled cry of anguish. Terrified eyes huge above her gag, Diana watched the two face each other.

'You really gonna brace me, saddle tramp?' Wes scoffed cockily.

'Go for your guns, or drop your gunbelt and put up your fists,' Matt challenged, his voice soft and scornful, arms loose at his sides.

Wes took a gunman's stance. He was a poised, coiled spring but something in the stranger's eyes told him this was not like facing down the ranch hands, dirt farmers, and drifters back in Willow Creek. Then he was bolstered by the other men's voices and footsteps.

'Thunderation,' Hiram Trask bellowed, halting in mid-step as he saw the two men squared off and the tied and gagged woman on the ground.

'I was about to put this grub-line rider in his place, Pa,' Wes said arrogantly.

'Your son is in for a bad beating, or he's a dead man if he pulls his guns. I'm no trick shot artist, when I shoot I aim to kill, not wing a man.'

'Slap leather, and you'll have me and my men throwing down on you, too.'

'Maybe so, but I'll take both you and your son with me before I fall,' Matt said, his tone cool and deadly. 'And that's a promise, not a threat.'

Hiram Trask knew men, and he knew damn well that the tall stranger wasn't running a bluff. 'Let's all simmer down a minute,' he said, trying to keep his voice controlled and reasonable. 'Now that the Utes are gone, there's no sense in anybody dying. What started this?'

'He was trying to take liberties with my girl. And you can see for yourself that she's not able to defend herself.'

Uncomfortable, Hiram Trask looked to his son and asked pointedly, 'That true, Wes?'

Wes hesitated, seeing the disapproval on his father's face and some of the others. 'I say she turned that murderer loose, and he tied and gagged her so it'd look right to us.'

'That's a filthy lie,' Matt cut in.

'Then how come she didn't scream or nothing while he was doing that to her!'

'Suppose someone removes her gag so she can say why,' Amos Long suggested from the back of the group.

'Whatever's said doesn't change what he was doing,' Matt said flatly.

'You're making such a fuss over a harmless little kiss,' Wes said with a forced lightness.

'You were planning to do more if I hadn't got here.'

'How do you know – are you a mind-reader?'

There was the sharp click of a shell being levered into the firing chamber of a Winchester and all eyes went to some rocks above and off to one side, near the horses, where Andy Denham stood covering the group. 'In case any of you cares,' he said almost matter-of-factly, 'the prisoner is still alive, and you can ask him too when he comes around.'

The news came as a surprise to everyone, but even more so to Jesse Seaton, who hid his true concern and asked, 'Are you sure, Andy?'

'Yeah, he's alive, just barely,' Andy confirmed. 'Now this disagreement can be settled later, when we're back in Willow Creek,' he said with a new-found authority. 'The Utes hear us killing one another and they'll come running back to see for themselves. And there's no time to be standing around watching any fist-fight. You all know we have

91

to dust out of here as fast as we can. We'll take our dead and bury them later. Some of you make a travois for the prisoner.'

Several groans went up, and Brick Calloway called, 'Leave 'im here for the Utes and let 'em finish the job.'

'He goes with us,' Andy said firmly, 'and that's final. This ain't a debating society.' He motioned with his rifle. 'C'mon, everybody get busy.' As the men dispersed, he looked to Matt and Wes, who turned away with a smug smile and strutted toward the horses. 'Sutton, as soon as you untie your girl, I want to see the both of you.'

CHAPTER ELEVEN

'Deputy, I did not set Rafe Lonis free,' Diana said earnestly, as she and Matt followed Andy Denham through the rocks.

'I know you didn't, ma'am,' Andy said reassuringly. 'And that's not what I wanted to talk to you folks about.' They came to the edge of the small clearing where Fowle lay dead and a townsman sat watching Rafe Lonis, propped against a boulder stained with his own blood, a torn white shirt across his chest. 'You can wait here if you want,' Andy said to Diana.

'I have seen dead and wounded men before.'

Andy gave a shrug. 'Suit yourself, ma'am.' He motioned. 'Come look at this.' He led the way to Fowle's body and knelt down, beckoning them to also do so. 'See that?' he said pointing.

Matt and Diana stared at slight, dark smudges on the shirt that were not completely hidden by blood. 'I'd say powder burns,' Matt said.

'And that's not all.' Andy took a .45 shell from his gunbelt and placed its tip over the entry wound. 'What do you say to that?'

'The hole's not big enough,' Matt said. 'More likely a .44.'

'Lonis had your gun, a .45. And he was standing too far away to give Fowle those powder burns.' Andy replaced the shell in a loop on his gunbelt, then dug into a pants pocket and withdrew a spent slug. 'This is what took Lonis down.'

'A .44,' Matt said, eyeing the twisted metal.

'Kinda strange, since Fowle had a rifle.'

'But why would someone shoot both men?' Diana asked.

'Orin Fowle was the only witness against Lonis,' Andy replied. 'And just suppose he really saw somebody else leaving Hobson's place, and was going to change his testimony.'

'That's possible,' Matt allowed.

'Why are you telling us this?' Diana asked, frowning curiously.

'You're the only ones not from Willow Creek, so you don't have a real interest in what happened there. Sure, you've got a grudge against Lonis for all what he done to both of you, but you didn't even know Fowle. Besides, I know where the two of you were during the fight with the Utes.'

'Then you believe that Lonis is innocent?' Diana said, encouraged that someone else now might honestly share her feeling about the man.

'I don't see why anyone in the posse would deal out vigilante justice except Elijah Hobson, and even so he'd have no call to shoot Fowle if he was a witness.'

'Maybe it was the other way around,' Matt

suggested, 'and Lonis blundered in and saw Fowle being killed.'

Andy shrugged. 'Either way, I believe the real killer of Miz Hobson is in this posse. And he'll try to finish the job on Lonis to protect himself. About half the men here have .44s, so the question is: how to smoke him out?'

'What do you want of us?' Diana asked.

'I ain't got the authority to deputize you, so all I can do is ask for your help. I'd like you to look after the prisoner till we get to town – if he manages to live that long. I don't trust anyone in the posse to do it, and I can't spend all my time on him.'

'We hadn't planned on going all the way to Willow Creek,' Matt said hesitantly. 'It's out of our way.'

'With the Utes stirred up, I'd say you ain't got much choice.' Andy smiled mirthlessly. 'Besides, don't you want a crack at Wes Trask? I'd give a pretty to see you lambaste him good. No shooting, mind you. We're already settin' on a powder keg as it is.'

Matt made no reply. He was mentally debating the choices. Here they were getting dragged into something that was none of their affair. Yet they were stuck with the posse, leastways until they were safely out of Ute territory, so they might as well try to do some good. And from the way Diana was looking at him, even though she wasn't putting in her two cents, he knew he'd never hear the end of it if they pulled out before the killer was unmasked.

'I reckon we'll stay a spell,' Matt drawled, trying to hide his reluctance. He saw Diana's face light up, pleased with his decision, and felt good all over – until he remembered there was an unknown killer in their midst who could strike without warning at any time.

The posse resumed their homeward journey with Rafe Lonis, alive but in a coma, pulled behind the pack horse on a travois and Fowle and the other dead man slung across their saddles. There were no more signs of the Utes but all threw wary glances behind from time to time, and there were plenty of complaints at their slow speed because of the wounded prisoner. Andy silenced them all; his secret knowledge that there was a killer amongst them and the fact that only Matt Sutton had backed him up during the attempt to hang Lonis gave him a contempt for the whole lot.

Sundown came but the group pushed on, guided by the stars. Finally they were thought to be out of Ute country and a halt was called. Still, that didn't mean the Utes wouldn't come after them if they took a mind to do so.

'Since Fowle and Crowe had no kin that we know about,' Andy said to the weary group, 'they won't be missed none in Boot Hill. We'd best plant them here and now, and be done with it.' His words met with disgruntled grumbles.

'Neither of them smelled like roses when they were alive,' Wes Trask piped up, 'and by tomorrow they'll stink like a passel of skunks.' His words brought hoots and laughter from the ranch hands.

'I'm ashamed for you, Wes,' Brick Calloway said, in mock seriousness. 'Ain't you got no respect for the dead?'

'I didn't have none whilst they were living,' Wes said. 'Why should I now, just 'cause they're dead?'

'Yeah, everybody becomes a saint when he's dead,' Brick said.

'Since you boys are having such a high ol' time entertaining yourselves,' Andy cut in, 'you can continue to do so while you dig – and that goes for you too, Wes.'

Wes opened his mouth to protest but Hiram Trask jumped in sternly. 'You heard the deputy. Get 'er done!'

Taking shovels from the pack horse, Wes and Brick alternated digging graves with two other ranch hands. Seaton and Elijah Hobson stood guard against any surprise attack, and Diana and Amos Long cooked over a camp-fire while Matt and Andy kept cautious eyes on Rafe Lonis, who remained in a coma.

When the graves were ready, Matt left Diana to watch Lonis and took over guard duty so Hobson and Seaton could pay their last respects. The bodies were placed in the ground, and since neither man was much liked and no one wished to be the centre of attention by saying hypocritical things about their virtues, the men merely bowed their heads for a moment of silent prayer.

To anyone who cared to notice, Hobson's grim face seemed fitting for paying his last respects to a neighbour. In reality he was once again mulling over the coincidence that the only witness of sorts and the man who supposedly murdered his wife and unborn child should meet and shoot each other. He was still pondering when the service ended and the graves were hastily filled in. He even helped place rocks on them to keep coyotes and other varmints from desecrating the bodies.

The buryings had put the men in a sombre, reflective mood, each man aware of his own mortality, and supper was eaten in near silence. Afterwards the camp-fire was snuffed with dirt and they pushed on. It was the custom with cautious travellers on the frontier to eat and then move on to another area before making camp for the night, as the smoke and camp-fire could be seen and smelled for miles out on the plains and might invite unwanted guests, both human and animal.

All were swaying wearily in their saddles when a halt was finally called in a jumble of rocks that afforded excellent protection for what remained of the night. Amid grumblings, a guard was posted, the men rotating each hour. Unknown to the others, Matt, Diana and Andy Denham kept their own secret watch over Rafe Lonis. There was no telling who the unknown killer was or when he might make a try to silence Lonis; he could even be one of the men taking a turn standing guard.

CHAPTER TWELVE

The night passed without incident, neither the Utes nor the unknown killer made an appearance, and Matt, Diana and Andy Denham only lost a few hours of sleep apiece.

'I'd say our man is biding his time and waiting to see if Lonis dies before we reach Willow Creek,' Matt said, letting his gaze wander seemingly casually over the men as they began to break camp.

'How far is that?' Diana asked Andy.

'At the slow rate we're travelling,' the deputy replied, 'I'd say maybe early tomorrow night.'

'Then he can bide his time and not make a move until we are near town,' Diana said, her eyes also roving over the group for a likely suspect.

'Unless Lonis becomes conscious enough to talk,' Matt said.

Andy turned to Diana. 'That's why I'd like you to stick right with him, ma'am. Just in case that does happen.'

Diana started to speak but caught herself as Hiram Trask, his son, and his ranch hands stomped up. She remained seated beside Rafe Lonis, who lay on his unhitched travois: a blanket stretched between two long pieces of wood. Matt and Andy stood and faced the men.

'You have something to say, do you, Mr Trask?' Andy said, with a lazy, strained politeness.

'A trial was held,' Hiram Trask stated stiffly, 'and that murderer was sentenced to hang. Sutton there prevented it from happening—'

'The Utes had a little something to do with that as well,' Andy interjected.

Trask frowned his annoyance and pressed on. 'Later, due to this young lady's apparent negligence, he almost escaped.'

'He probably would have,' Wes put in, 'if Orin Fowle hadn't stopped him – and got hisself killed in the bargain.'

'Is this gonna be a stem-winder,' Andy said, 'or do you have a point to make?'

'The point is,' Hiram Trask fired back, 'instead of toting this killer back to town at a snail's pace, we oughta string him up here and now – whether he's conscious or not.' Wes and the others seconded his words.

'That's barbaric!' Diana cried.

'He's in no shape to escape or do anybody any harm,' Andy said flatly, 'so he's going to Willow Creek for trial, if he survives the journey.' His eyes moved over the sullen faces. 'That's the way it was supposed to be in the first place. The circuit judge can decide things, nice and legal-like.' There was a long silence. The men made no move to leave. 'The Utes are no longer a threat,' Andy added. 'Anybody

100

got urgent business in town, he's free to ride on.'

The men looked to Hiram Trask, awaiting his decision. 'I'll think on it,' he said at last and turned away. The others started to follow, but suddenly Rafe Lonis stirred and moaned loudly. The men whirled back.

'Aw hell,' Wes said, 'that's downright pitiful. He's gotta be put outta his misery.' His hand flashed to his gun, and to his group the draw was greased lightning. But no sooner did he clear his holster than the barrel of Matt's heavy .45 sliced down on his wrist. Wes howled his pain and clutched his throbbing wrist as the gun leaped from his numb fingers and fell to the ground. 'You like to busted my wrist, you bas—' he began angrily.

The sentence went unfinished as, with a seemingly effortless movement, Matt slammed his gun barrel against the side of Wes Trask's head. Wes careered backwards, unconscious, into Brick and they went down in an ungainly tangle of arms and legs. Matt trained his weapon on the others and asked, low and deadly, 'Anyone else feeling frisky?'

The men were properly cowed. Seaton, Hobson, Amos Long and the few saloon toughs came drifting over to see what was up.

'Trask, you're through making big tracks with this posse,' Andy said, meeting the older man's flinty eyes with an equal hardness. 'If you stay, you and your men take my orders and that's final.'

'You're suddenly rearing up on your high horse now, aren't you, Denham?' Trask rasped. 'Well, enjoy yourself, because that gunslinger won't be siding you for ever. And you won't have a job when we get back to town.' He turned his harsh gaze on Matt, who was holstering his six-gun. 'Willow Creek is posted to you, Sutton. That goes for your woman, too. So there's no call to stay with this posse any longer.'

'That's enough, Trask,' Andy snapped. 'I said you were through giving orders here. Until Sheriff Crandall is on his feet again, I'm the law in Willow Creek. Start any trouble and you and your whole lot will join this prisoner in jail. '

'I've had my say,' Trask said, unperturbed, 'and I've given fair warning: Willow Creek doesn't need the three of you.' With that he turned on his heel and strode away, his back stiff as a ramrod. His men followed, Brick and another man dragging Wes Trask's limp body between them, the toes of his boots cutting twin furrows in the dirt.

'I don't know as that was such a wise thing to do, Andy,' Amos Long said, and shook his head.

'Trask means it about your job,' Jesse Seaton added. 'Maybe if I talk to him after he's had a chance to cool off some.'

'Thanks, but I've had a bellyful of taking Trask's orders, even if Sheriff Crandall hasn't.'

'Those are proud words right now,' Seaton pressed, 'but they don't put money in your pocket – and you might not be able to get another job in Willow Creek.'

Andy remained stubbornly silent. The men walked off, and he turned to Matt. 'Regardless what happens later, it was all worth it to see you lay Wes Trask low in the dust.' He smiled. 'Sorta evens things for that knock on the head he gave me up on the mountain.'

His expression became serious. 'Watch yourself from now on, you've made some powerful enemies.'

'I'd say that goes for you too,' Matt said. He let a half-smile cross his weathered features. 'We're in pretty good company, huh?'

'Damn straight,' Andy replied, and grinned.

The posse was preparing to leave when Wes Trask and Brick Calloway reined in near where Matt and Diana were checking the saddles on their mounts. Wes sat glaring down as Matt paid him no mind, then finally called irritably, 'I'm leaving now, Sutton. Pa's staying on, just so's you and that poor excuse for a deputy don't try to hog the *glory* of catching that killer for your lonesomes.' He again waited. And again he was ignored. Shifting about in the saddle, he then said harshly, 'Pa wasn't joshing about you keeping out of Willow Creek. But if you've a mind to commit suicide, you come ahead on and show us you ain't yellow. I'll be waiting for you.' He flashed a cocky grin and looked to Diana. 'There'll be a more friendly reception for you, sugar. You'll really enjoy our down-home hospitality, as they say, in your Rebel land.'

'Yes, ma'am,' Brick interjected snidely.

The men waited, hoping there would be some response to their taunts. But Matt and Diana had learned long ago that silence was a far greater rejoinder than any verbal reply. Wes Trask's expression became hard and he jerked his horse's head up and spurred away. Brick Calloway gigged his mount after him.

'White trash scum,' Diana said, staring after them. Turning to Matt, she said, concerned, 'There will be shooting if we do go into Willow Creek.'

Matt nodded, then shrugged. 'If Lonis dies before we get there, or else we flush out the real killer, there'll be no reason to even go into that town.'

'And if neither thing happens?'

'We'll just have to wait and see.' Matt rammed a boot into a stirrup and swung aboard his horse. He waited for Diana to mount then they headed after the departing posse.

CHAPTER THIRTEEN

The day passed without incident. Matt Sutton and Andy Denham received dark looks from Hiram Trask and his remaining ranch hands but there were no verbal exchanges. For the most part, the posse rode in stony silence. Rafe Lonis remained in his semi-conscious state, murmuring incoherently on occasion but not responding to Diana's gentle urgings to tell who had shot him.

Hiram Trask was not used to having his authority challenged, particularly by a young deputy who had been lackadaisical in his job at best, until he teamed up with that drifter and his woman. Why those two stayed and even protected Rafe Lonis, especially after he'd stolen the girl (Trask could not fault Lonis for that, as the blonde was indeed a real looker) and had left the man to take his place as a fugitive, was beyond the old rancher. Hoping to avoid further trouble with Sutton, Trask had sent Wes on to town. The boy was headstrong and his pride had been hurt bad so he was still spoiling for a fight. Trask hoped to hell Lonis would die before they reached Willow Creek, then Sutton and the woman could bypass the town completely and go on their way. If not, then he'd have to take steps to protect his son, who was clearly no match for the experienced gunman. Just what that would be, Trask had no idea. But he would do whatever was necessary when the time came.

Cold and withdrawn, Elijah Hobson surreptitiously studied everyone but Matt and Diana from time to time, hoping to somehow glean which one was the guilty party. Even Andy Denham was not completely free from Hobson's suspicion. Though he tried to reassure himself that Rafe Lonis was indeed the man responsible for his tragedy, his mind now no longer blindly accepted that without question. Hobson found himself willing the man not to die, at least until he had revealed the true killer.

Matt, Diana, and Andy were also trying to watch the various men's movements. It was still light so nothing was bound to happen yet. The slow travel because of Lonis's travois meant they would not reach Willow Creek until well into the night, and so the three had to keep a strict vigil from sunset on.

Seeing Andy's worried face, Matt remarked, 'There's no call to be fretting this early. I doubt our man's gonna do anything till night, if then.'

'My concern is that this won't be over when the prisoner is in the jailhouse,' Andy said sombrely. 'In fact it won't be over until the circuit judge holds court and passes sentence, one way or the other – if there's not a lynching before he arrives.'

'Been many lynchings in Willow Creek?'

'A few legal hangings, but no lynchings. But then, there's never been a crime like this before. People will be pretty riled, 'specially if the Trasks start egging on the saloon soldiers and others.'

'You'd best telegraph for the county sheriff.'

'I know it's asking a lot, but would you be willing to stay on until I can get some kind of help?'

'I'm no lawman. And you heard Trask. My staying would only make things worse.'

'Maybe you're right,' Andy allowed reluctantly. 'Besides, it ain't your fight. You've done more than enough already, what with catching him and all.'

'I had a vested interest – clearing myself and getting Diana back safe and undamaged.'

'Reckon you did, at that.'

'Anyway, let's not go getting headaches ahead of time. Things might just work themselves out to everybody's satisfaction.'

Andy forced a smile and nodded, trying to find some assurance in Matt's words. Still, he damned fate for sticking him with this thankless job to begin with.

The sun was sinking, pitching sharply toward the horizon and turning the clouds pink and grey. Elongated shadows began to merge with the encroaching darkness that was slowly dropping over the rimtops.

This was what Jesse Seaton had been wating patiently for throughout the seemingly endless daylight hours. When it was finally full dark, he would have to find the right opportunity to strike without being seen. That was a tall order, as the girl was with Rafe Lonis almost constantly, as well as Sutton and Andy Denham. Seaton guessed that he had a good four or so more hours in which to act, thanks to their slow pace. It would be so much simpler if the man died on his own before they reached town – and without first regaining consciousness. For about the hundredth time he cursed both his aim and his stupidity for not putting another bullet or two in Lonis to ensure that he was dead. Because of that blunder he would now have to risk exposure to finish the job.

Seaton was so deep in brooding thought that he did not hear Andy Denham's order to halt for a rest and to eat supper. It wasn't until Amos Long shouted to him that he turned in the saddle and saw the men dismounting. He wheeled around and rode back, grinning sheepishly. Dismounting, he watched the men mill about in small groups and tried to avoid being drawn into one, as there would be no chance to make a move if Lonis was left briefly unguarded. A minute at the most was all he needed to end the man's life once and for all.

Luck favoured Seaton. When he hobbled his horse with Long's and several others, he noticed that Elijah Hobson had left a saddle-bag pocket open and a Bowie knife with his initials on the hilt was partly revealed inside. He filched the knife and, hiding it under his coat, walked away casually. He passed near where Hiram Trask and his 'punchers were building a cooking fire. There was none of the usual good-natured joshing; instead, the men cast sullen looks toward Andy and Matt who were tending their horses. Seaton skirted around, staying in the shadows, and came up in the rocks only yards from where the girl was nursing the wounded, delirious prisoner. Seaton settled down and waited. Then, again, luck came his way.

Andy walked up with Matt and said to Diana, 'Why don't you get something to eat and visit a spell with Matt. You been with the prisoner for most of the day.'

Diana nodded and smiled gratefully. 'Thank you, Andy. I could use a rest.' She stood and stretched, rubbing the small of her back, then walked off with Matt.

Andy stared after the two, then sat beside the still hitched up travois, with his back to the rocks. He looked down at Lonis and muttered, 'If you knew all the grief and misery you was causing folks, you'd wake right up from there and tell us all who really shot you.'

Seaton tensed in his hiding place. He'd never suspected that anyone knew Lonis had not been shot by Fowle. Now it was even more imperative that he finish the job on Lonis as quickly as possible. He waited restlessly while the deputy settled into a comfortable position, his back still toward the rocks, then quietly picked up a rock and weighed it in his hand. Satisfied that it was suitable for the job, he eased himself up and crept forward on cat's feet.

Andy detected a sound behind him too late. He started to turn his head but something very hard crashed down on top of his head and his Stetson gave little protection. Stars and rockets burst before his eyes, then everything turned grey, and blackness took him.

Discarding the rock, Seaton pulled the Bowie

knife from inside his coat and stepped over Andy's sprawled body. The horse whinnied and moved forward in its hobbles, pulling the travois with it. Seaton cursed and muttered soothingly to the animal as he was forced to follow and position himself directly over the prisoner. He raised the knife and prepared to strike.

Suddenly the girl screamed. Then a gunshot shattered the blade, and sent the knife leaping from his hand.

Startled, Seaton whirled and dove into the rocks. Another shot showered bits of rock and debris over him as, crouched low, he weaved hurriedly through the shadowy maze. Behind him there was a mad commotion: shouts, running footsteps, and horses whinnying and stamping. Seaton broke from the rocks and circled around, unseen, to come up beside Amos Long.

'What's all the fuss, Amos?' Seaton enquired innocently, striving to keep the previous exertion from his voice.

'I don't know,' Long answered. 'Maybe someone tried to kill the prisoner.'

'Could be,' Seaton said easily. 'He's not exactly popular with most of us.' They walked on to join the crowd that had formed around the travois.

'He dead?' Hiram Trask asked, his voice unconcerned, as Matt knelt and checked Andy.

'Just knocked on the head,' Matt replied. 'Hat helped some . . . but he's got a lump as big as a goose egg.' Andy groaned and showed signs of regaining consciousness.

'Matt, look at this,' Diana said. She picked up the broken knife and walked to him, holding out its hilt.

'E. H.,' Matt read aloud. He looked about at the faces in the crowd and asked, 'Anybody know who that is?' At first his question was met with only sullen silence, then a 'puncher spoke up.

'Elijah Hobson is about the only one here with them initials.' Several other men voiced their agreement.

'If it was him,' Hiram Trask said sternly, 'nobody can fault him one bit.' Again, there were agreeing voices.

'Where is Hobson, anyway?' Amos Long asked. The crowd murmured and looked about for him.

Diana wet a bandanna from a canteen and bathed Andy's grimy face as he moaned and stirred. Matt set down the knife and raised him up to a half-sitting position, braced on an elbow.

'My aching head,' the deputy said, wincing as he touched the lump carefully with his fingertips. 'I swear to goodness I'm gonna become the town half-wit if this don't stop.'

Matt held up three fingers and asked, 'How many fingers you see?'

Andy's dazed eyes focused slowly and he replied, 'Three.'

Matt nodded. 'You're seeing things fine.'

Andy gave a sudden start, remembering. 'The prisoner?'

'Still breathing,' Matt replied.

'Too bad,' Trask said, and others agreed.

'Did you see who hit you, Andy?' Seaton asked in

his best concerned manner.

'Didn't see a thing,' Andy said. He shook his head and immediately regretted it, gasping and grimacing with pain.

Seaton felt the tension that he'd been hiding inside relax. He had failed in his task but at least it appeared that Hobson would take the blame, as he'd planned.

'Here's Hobson now,' a ranch hand announced.

Elijah Hobson approached from the direction of some rocks and bushes on the other side of camp. He scowled, puzzled, as all eyes watched him. 'What's everybody looking at?' he demanded gruffly. Men gave way for him and he strode up to the travois, looked down at Lonis, then across to Andy, Matt and Diana. 'Did somebody do him?' he asked, gesturing at Lonis, who was lying still.

'Somebody hit me and tried to,' Andy answered. 'Where have you been?'

Hobson hesitated and glanced uncomfortably at Diana, then down at the ground.

'The deputy asked you a question, Hobson,' Trask said. Other men urged Hobson for an answer.

'You'd best answer him, Elijah,' Seaton prompted. 'If you're innocent there's no concern. If not, all the deputy has against you is a lumpy head.' That brought laughs from some of the men, as Seaton had hoped.

'Let's have it, Hobson,' Andy said, struggling to his feet, aided by Matt.

'I . . .' Hobson began, averting his eyes from Diana. 'I was answering the call of nature, damn you.' His face flushed with embarrassment. The men laughed uproariously at his discomfort.

When the laughter had died down, Trask asked, 'What about you and your woman, Sutton? She screamed and you did some shooting.'

A brief glance passed between the two, then Matt said, 'He was too far away and in the shadows.'

'That's right,' Diana seconded.

Andy picked up the broken knife and held it out to Hobson. 'This is your knife, ain't it?'

'I had it in my saddle-bags. Somebody musta stole it.'

'If somebody did take it,' Seaton said easily, 'I'm sure he's not going to admit it.'

Andy expelled his breath in a heavy sigh and handed the broken knife to Hobson, who looked at it than flipped it casually into the rocks where it clattered metallically and was silent. Though he didn't feel much like it, as his head was throbbing and buzzing like a beehive, Andy summoned an authoritative tone.

'Aw right, let's break camp and move on. There'll only be short breaks from now on till we reach Willow Creek.' As the men started to turn away, he added sharply, 'Anybody but me, Sutton, and his lady comes near the prisoner then, no questions asked, he gets shot. I mean it now. None of you got any call to do so.'

There were a few dirty looks but no one challenged him and the group drifted off. 'A couple of teacher's pets,' a 'puncher remarked and some of the men laughed.

Andy watched them go and, when they were out of earshot, he turned to Matt and Diana. 'You folks honestly didn't see the man good?'

'No, we didn't,' Diana responded.

'But whoever he was,' Matt added, 'he wasn't as big as Hobson.'

'So he was telling the truth about his knife being stolen, huh?'

'Yeah,' Matt agreed.

'At least we know the real murderer is still with the posse,' Diana said quietly, staring after the dispersing men.

'Reckon so,' Andy said, then managed a weak grin. 'I'm kinda sorry about that. Here I was hoping it would be Wes Trask.' He set his hat carefully atop his head. 'Whenever that *hombre*'s found, I'm gonna collect for this knot on my head.'

CHAPTER FOURTEEN

A myriad of twinkling stars lighting their way, the posse rode across the semi-desert landscape at as brisk a pace as it was deemed the wounded man could stand. Not taking Andy Denham's warning lightly, the strung-out riders kept their distance from the travois, its horse's reins held by the deputy, while Matt Sutton rode on one side, positioned between it and the men, and Diana Logan brought up the rear, keeping a careful eye on the unconscious prisoner. Each mile took them closer to Willow Creek, and the killer's time to again act was slowly running out like the sand in an hourglass.

No one was more aware of that fact than Jesse Seaton. There was no longer hope of getting at Rafe Lonis unnoticed as long as Denham and his two unofficial deputies, Sutton and his woman, watched over him like mother hens. At least, he was still in the clear, and maybe he could still do something when they reached town. And, of course, there was always the possibility that the prisoner would die before they got there.

Then Seaton remembered Hiram Trask's warning to Sutton about staying out of Willow Creek. From what he'd seen, Sutton didn't appear to be a man who would back down. Chances were he'd go right to the jailhouse with the prisoner. And chances were, Hiram Trask wouldn't stand still for his authority to be challenged in *his* town by a stranger. He would have to assert himself. And with Trask's hotheaded son, Wes, there could well be shooting. During the ensuing gunplay a stray shot, fired supposedly by one of the participants, would end Rafe Lonis's life. This time Seaton would see that it happened. He rode on, smiling to himself and envisioning the gunfight. Should both Trasks be taken down it would leave a void in the town's leadership that he would gladly fill.

Elijah Hobson was not a thinking man. He was blunt and to the point. Still, he'd done more than his share of pondering ever since they had started back to town with the prisoner. And he had come to the obvious conclusion that they had the wrong man. If some public-minded person wanted to take justice into his own hands, why in hell would he go to the bother of stealing the knife from his saddle-bags? No, the real killer was amongst the posse, and he'd meant to cover his tracks and leave Hobson to take the blame. After all, who'd have more reason to kill the prisoner than the grief-stricken husband of the murdered woman? Nobody would blame him, or even look any further. In spite of his vehement denial, Hobson bet about everyone in the posse still suspected him. Well, by the Lord Harry, he was going

116

to find the murderer and deal with him with his own bare hands – and it would not be an easy death.

The distant, brightly burning lights of Willow Creek brought a welcome relief to most, but to others they signalled the beginning of a new ordeal. It was then, with the journey almost completed, that Rafe Lonis died. As it had been with his life, no one was aware of his passing. The breath left his body in a long, soft sigh that went unnoticed, for it was at that exact moment Hiram Trask turned in his saddle and glowered across at Matt.

'There's the town, Sutton, your nurse-maiding work is done. It's still posted to you, so ride on now, if you know what's good for you.'

'I already told you, *Mister* Trask,' Andy spoke up before Matt could respond, 'that you're through telling folks what to do. Sutton and his lady are as welcome there as any other law-abiding folks. So suppose you and your lot ride on in ahead of us and let everybody know we're coming with the prisoner.'

'I'll send my boys ahead, but I'm riding right up to the jail with you,' Trask said flatly.

'Suit yourself,' Andy said, and gave an indifferent shrug.

The danger of a flare-up past, Diana returned her attention to Rafe Lonis and became aware that he was lying too still and not breathing. Having seen dead men before, she kept her wits about her and, under the guise of straightening his blanket, checked his pulse and heartbeat surreptitiously for confirmation.

117

Sitting back, Diana felt a brief moment of pity for Rafe Lonis, but she had the presence of mind to realize that his death should be kept secret for as long as possible. There was still the hope that the real killer would reveal himself by making a last desperate attempt before they reached the sheriff's office. Then Andy Dehnam's voice calling a ten-minute rest broke into her thoughts and Diana turned to see Matt dismounting nearby. Rising, she forced a smile and moved to him with a seemingly casual, leggy stride.

Matt's face betrayed no emotion at the news, then he ambled back to Lonis's body with Diana. To anyone watching, the couple appeared to be in idle conversation. Andy Denham joined them presently and was informed of the prisoner's death.

'That tears it,' the deputy said disgustedly. 'Guess now we'll never know the truth.' He gave a heavy sigh. 'I hate the idea that a killer is gonna be living free and clear in Willow Creek but there's nothing to do about it.' He studied Matt earnestly. 'This releases you from any obligation. I'll take the body on into town.'

'We're the only ones who know what's happened.'

'That's right,' Diana quickly agreed.

'Yeah, but there ain't no sense in you bucking Hiram Trask and his men. He sure won't back down. He can't afford to or he'd lose face. By now that little weasel Wes has told the whole town about it being posted to you.' Just then the last of Hiram Trask's riders spurred away noisily toward town. As the three stared after them Andy added, 'And if Wes hasn't,

118

that bunch will.'

Matt and Diana exchanged grim, thoughtful glances. Both knew there was truth in what Andy had said, and the temptation to obey logic and light a shuck out of there was strong. After all, it wasn't their town, and certainly not really their affair. Yet the harsh memory of the personal misery brought on by the unknown killer framing Rafe Lonis, who had then involved them, swept aside all else.

'I've never run from trouble,' Matt said stolidly, 'and I'm not about to start now. Besides, we both owe this killer for what all we've been through – and I intend to pay him back for it more than double. Trask, his son, or any of his cowhands stand in the way and they'll sure wish they hadn't. Posted or not, I'm going in there.' Diana stepped to Matt's side, took his arm, and nodded her agreement.

Relief was plain on Andy Denham's face. He had no idea just how they would ferret out the killer, but he felt a whole lot more confident of success with Matt Sutton siding him. Quietly, he and the couple began to lay plans for the final stage of their journey and what they would do in Willow Creek.

At a corner table in the Long Trail Saloon, Wes Trask and Brick Calloway were told by the last of the Trask riders that the posse would soon be in town, and that the gunman and his woman were still with it.

'I am powerful pleased to hear that,' Wes said, and leaned back in his chair, a smile of pure malevolence on his face. 'You boys go have a few drinks on me at the bar.' As the men muttered their thanks and started to leave, Wes added as an afterthought, 'Don't abuse my hospitality now, hear? I want you sober and steady when the fireworks start.'

Agreeing, the men slouched off to the bar.

Brick eyed Wes and asked speculatively, 'You still of a mind to brace Sutton?'

'Hell, yes,' Wes replied without delay. 'Nobody can brace me like that and get away with it!'

'He coulda kilt you, and he didn't.'

'Too many Trask hands around. He'd have been ventilated so bad he'd whistle like a fife when the wind blowed.'

'That don't change the fact he's faster than you. Him and his lady got no reason to stay around once that killer's delivered to the jailhouse. They'll be gone by morning, so why hunt for trouble?'

'Pa posted this town to them.' Wes leaned forward and glared harshly at Brick. 'Are you going yellow on me?'

Undaunted, Brick said reasonably, 'Wes, I ride for the brand and I'm proud to do so . . . but this ain't ranch business. You and your pa should let the law handle things, and leave Sutton be unless he starts trouble on his own.'

'I am downright disappointed in you, Brick,' Wes said contemptuously. 'Men will be all along the street to the jail. There's no way Sutton will reach it. But if you're a-scared, maybe you oughta go back to the bunkhouse and hide under your bed till this is over.'

Brick tensed and flushed in anger, his jaw tight. Wisely, he made no response. He certainly didn't want to egg Wes into taking some of his building hatred out on him. The semblance of a strained smile crossing his weathered features, Brick pushed back his chair and rose to his feet. 'That's mighty good advice, Wes,' he said, his voice not quite achieving the casualness he'd wished. 'I think I'll do just that.'

'You do and you can pack your war bags and keep right on riding,' Wes said nastily. 'There's no place for cowards or shirkers on the Double Bar T.'

Though it was hard for a redheaded man to do so, Brick Calloway forced himself to disregard the stinging insult and the expectant eyes of the ranch hands and others in the saloon and turned and walked away. The abrupt quiet seemed to magnify his booted steps and jingling spurs as he strode across the sawdust floor.

Triumph feeding his bullying instincts, Wes pressed on cruelly, forgetting their former friendship of sorts 'That's right, Calloway. Slink on out of here with your tail betwixt your legs like an old yellow dog.'

Brick Calloway hesitated at the batwing doors as pride tried to have its way with him. With great difficulty, wisdom prevailed. He shoved through the swinging doors and stepped out into the cool night breeze, which did nothing to lessen his seething rage. As he stalked to his horse, standing hipshot at the nearest hitch rail, the lively music and voices resumed inside the saloon.

Untying the reins, Brick prepared to mount, but his rifle's stock jutting from its scabbard caught his eye enticingly. He shook his head and heaved a sigh of disgust, then rammed a boot into the stirrup and hauled himself aboard. He knew he wasn't a coward, and damned if he was gonna get killed trying to prove it to a bunch of saloon riff-raff.

As Brick trotted off along the street, a sudden inspiration broke through his dark thoughts. He knew what he had to do, and there was no living with himself if he didn't. Wrenching his horse's head around so hard the startled animal almost fell, Brick then put the spurs to it and galloped back the way he came.

CHAPTER FIFTEEN

Across the flat the nearing lights of Willow Creek began to dim as the posse approached. None of the raucous saloon sounds drifted out to them, and it appeared the town was closing up for the night.

'Way too early for the saloons to close,' Andy Denham remarked solemnly to Matt Sutton, riding beside him. 'I'd hoped folks would turn out to see us ride in with our man. Be less chance of trouble that way.'

'Maybe,' Matt responded flat-toned, 'but if trouble's bent on happening, there's no side-stepping it, crowd or no crowd.'

The group halted as the sound of racing hoofbeats reached them and a lone rider's dark shape was spotted, coming toward them hell for leather. Curious, apprehensive glances were exchanged by all as the horseman continued on relentlessly across the moon-splashed plain.

'Now who in hell is that?' Andy remarked, more to himself than to anyone in particular.

'The way he's running that horse,' Matt said, 'we'll know soon enough.'

Presently the rider's features were visible, and Andy announced, 'It's Brick Calloway.' The frothy, racing horse slid to a quick stop before Matt and Andy.

'What are you doing here, Calloway?' Hiram Trask called.

Ignoring the question, Brick addressed Matt. 'You're up against a stacked deck. Wes Trask has men lined up on both sides of Main Street. You and the prisoner ain't gonna reach the jail in one piece.'

'Calloway, you're fired, you damn turncoat,' Hiram Trask exploded.

'Your son already done that, Trask. I'm here to salve my own conscience.'

'*Mister* to you, cowhand.'

'You and Wes ain't high in my esteem no more,' Brick said and shook his head. Then he took petty delight in adding, 'Dry-gulching is for snakes and lesser varmints.'

'Nobody dares talk to me like that,' Trask shouted, nearly apoplectic.

'I just did. You want ta hear it again, *Trask*?'

Trembling with rage at the public affront to his dignity by a lowly cowboy, Hiram Trask whipped his hand to his holster. Matt cleared leather before the older man had his Colt halfway out.

'Pull that six-gun and I'll blast you out of your saddle,' Matt said, his voice sharp and deadly. 'A bullet don't give a damn how big or small you stand in the community.'

Trask checked his movement and let the pistol slip back into its holster then sat scowling and fuming inwardly.

'Thanks,' Brick said to Matt.

'Just returning the favour,' Matt said easily, and they exchanged grins. 'It appears you've burned your bridges here.'

Brick shrugged. 'Makes no difference, I'm pulling out tonight. This ain't my quarrel. Good luck to you and your lady, Sutton.' He turned his mount and cantered away, riding well clear of the town.

The posse stared after the departing horseman for a long while, then Andy Denham said loudly, 'Aw right, let's git,' and gigged his horse forward.

Like a general marshalling his troops, Wes Trask scattered his ten ranch hands in dark alleys, windows, and tops of buildings along Main Street. Yes, sir, Sutton would run one helluva gauntlet to reach the jail. It would be nothing short of a miracle if he somehow survived. Also, in the midst of the shooting, there was a very real chance that a stray bullet would finish off the prisoner, and then justice would be served without further delay. Wes grinned. It was sorta nice to be a public-spirited citizen.

The posse halted at the city limits sign that stated Willow Creek's population was 525, which would have to be revised to account for those lost in the Indian fight, and possibly even more, should the impending shoot-out still occur.

'I'm sorry, Andy,' Amos Long said sheepishly, 'but I can't go any further.' Then he added defensively, 'I've fulfilled my—'

'That's all right, Amos,' the deputy interrupted

understandingly. He looked about at the others. 'I can't ask none of you to ride down that street.'

All eyes studied the dark street for signs of life. The few lanterns along the length of the street had been extinguished, as had those in the various saloons. Horses were gone from the hitch rails and not a soul stirred on the street. Still, the omnious silence seemed a living thing.

'Trask, you can stop this, if you've a mind,' Andy said.

'My boy's doing what's right,' the older man replied flatly.

'Any shooting starts and I'm holding you responsible.'

'*If* you and your gunhawk come through it.'

'That goes for you, too. You're riding right alongside of us, all the way to the jail. And if I go down so will you. That's a statement of fact.'

'And I damn well guarantee it, old man,' Matt put in.

'The both of you can go straight to hell,' Hiram Trask snapped and sat his horse arrogantly, undaunted by the men's harsh stares.

This was the opportunity Jesse Seaton had awaited, and he seized it straight away. 'Let me try to reason with Wes,' he said in his best peacemaking tone, 'and perhaps trouble can be avoided.'

Andy glanced to Matt, who considered and nodded his agreement, then back to Seaton. 'All right, Jesse, but impress on Wes that he'll be an orphan if there's any shooting.'

'I will,' Seaton said solemnly and put his horse

forward at a walk.

Andy turned and addressed the few remaining possemen. 'Everybody's discharged. Turn in your vouchers tomorrow, and Sheriff Crandall will see to them as soon as he's able.' The men dispersed hurriedly, even Elijah Hobson, which was secretly a relief, as it was easier to keep up the pretence of Rafe Lonis being alive.

Midway along the street, Jesse Seaton was seen halting beside a hotel. He dismounted, left his horse at the tie rack and entered the shadowy doorway. Matt, Diana, Andy and the older Trask waited tensely, straining keenly to see and hear what was being said, even though the distance was too great.

Finally Seaton emerged from the hotel and called, 'It's all set. Wes agrees there'll be no trouble. Go on to the sheriff's office and I'll join you there later.' He moved to his horse, took down his rifle and saddle-bags, and went back into the hotel.

The group hesitated, waiting for Wes and the ranch hands to show themselves. None did. Scowling, Matt glanced over at Diana. 'Just the same, maybe you'd best wait.'

'There will be even less chance of shooting if I'm with you,' Diana said firmly.

'She's right,' Hiram Trask said self-righteously, 'we Trasks don't wage war on women.'

'Anything goes wrong, Trask, you and your son are dead men,' Matt warned icily. 'Now lead off.'

Trask obeyed and, gunhands resting on the handles of their six-guns, Matt and Andy trailed behind, their wary eyes sweeping the sides of the street and building tops. Still leading the horse pulling Lonis's travois, Diana followed after the men. Despite the apparent truce, the only sounds were the dull thud of their horses' hoofs, jingling of bridles, creaking of saddle leather, and the travois poles dragging along the hard ground.

After collecting his room key, Jesse Seaton left Wes Trask in the hotel lobby and went up the flight of stairs to the second-floor room that had been his before his marriage of convenience and was now kept, not only for those times he honestly worked late in his office and did not care to make the two-mile ride to the mansion he shared with his wife, but when he just plain did not want to be in her company.

Emerging from the empty hallway, Seaton dropped his saddle-bags by the door but kept the Winchester and, not lighting a lamp, let the bright moonlight guide him to a window overlooking Main Street. He eased it open quietly, then stepped to one side and stood in the darkness with his rifle ready, waiting for the riders to pass.

Tonight Trask rule would be broken for ever, and he would become the new town boss.

Cussing a blue-streak under his breath, Wes Trask slipped out the side door of the hotel and strode to Chuck Rand, a beefy, sour-faced cowhand, who stood with his six-gun drawn. 'That damn, no-account Brick Calloway told 'em of my trap,' he informed the man. 'I'll settle his hash later – but good!'

'Never did cotton much to him, anyways,' Rand commented in a gravelly voice.

'No two-bit gunman and a tin star deputy who's suddenly got religion are gonna dictate to me and Pa.'

'You still aimin' to go through with it?'

'Damn straight. There's bound to be a moment before they reach the jail when my pa will have a chance to make a break. When that happens, shoot – but be careful not to hit the girl. Later, we'll have lotsa good fun tormenting her.'

The two grinned wickedly, then Rand said, 'I think I can cut her out for us. Want me to try?'

Wes nodded and grinned widely as a plan came to him. 'Yeah, you do that, Chuck, and it'll be our signal to start something so Pa can make his break.'

Making a break was something Hiram Trask wished to do very badly, but he was held in a grip of fear. He had been threatened many times in the past; some of the men just made angry talk while others meant it but lacked the skill to put their woes into actions successfully. Now, for the first time, Trask had met someone with the skill and resolve to carry out the threat and he realized there was a very real chance of dying. Young or old, a man longs to cling to every second of life for as long as he can.

Trask kept a tight rein on his horse, just as he'd been ordered, and prayed that his impulsive son wouldn't go and do something stupid that would get him killed. Though he couldn't see them, he knew Wes and the ranch hands were hiding out there in the shadows and darkness on both sides of the quiet street. Both knew it was bad business to let a drifting stranger successfully challenge Trask authority.

Others, like that fool deputy, would start getting ideas, and if the sheep of the town ever took a notion to unite there would be real trouble. Some way the situation had to be turned around – and before this night was up.

As though they hadn't a care in the world, the woman and two men rode leisurely behind Hiram Trask. Their attention was on gaining the relative safety of the darkened sheriff's office that was only six long blocks ahead, but appeared to be a million miles away. They could feel the unseen hostile eyes watching their slow progress along the wide street. By now the whole town knew that the posse had returned with the killer, and the trick was to get the dead man inside the jail without anyone spotting the ruse.

Diana's eyes remained straight ahead, watching Hiram Trask, and also for any sudden danger that might crop up in that direction. Andy concentrated his attention on the shadowy doorways and alleys along the left side of the street while Matt watched the right side, including rooftops. Nothing stirred, and it seemed they might just reach their destination without any trouble.

Jesse Seaton saw the riders slowly approaching the hotel and edged back deeper into the shadows of his room. Then he moved quickly and silently to the other side of the open window, so that he could fire after the group had passed the hotel and none would see the flash from his Winchester. Despite the cool breeze fluttering the curtains slightly, he was sweating and could feel a nervous tremor that he had to bring under control if he was to accomplish his goal.

Slowly, ever so slowly, the riders went by. Seaton brought the rifle to his shoulder and started to take aim. There was a moment of indecision as he pondered whether Hiram Trask or the wounded prisoner should be his first shot. Logic dictated that he shoot Rafe Lonis, ending any fear he would awaken and tell what he'd heard and seen. Of course, it would be the word of a killer against that of the town's highly respected lawyer, but why allow any room for doubt to creep into the townspeople's minds?

Seaton knelt and, careful to keep the muzzle inside the room so it wouldn't be seen, took aim at the man on the slow-moving travois. His finger tightened on the trigger – and then something very unexpected happened.

CHAPTER SIXTEEN

There was a sudden *whoosh* of air as a lariat sailed out from the dark alley beside the hotel and settled around Diana Logan's torso, pinning her arms to her sides. A swift yank hurled her from the saddle and her startled cry was cut abruptly as she crashed to the ground on her back and the wind was driven from her slender body. Semi-conscious, she was dimly aware of being drawn rapidly along the ground to the nearby alley.

Both Diana's mare and the horse pulling the travois shied and whinnied, startled. And at that moment a rifle shot smashed into one of the travois's wooden poles, and its ear-splitting sound ignited a powder keg of brutal violence.

Simultaneously swivelling in the saddle and drawing his gun, Matt saw Diana's limp form being dragged into the dark alley. He threw a shot, but from his angle the bullet only gouged splinters from the corner of a dry goods store next to hotel. Then the street was filled with gunfire and bullets rained all around him, one slamming into his saddle horn while another sent his hat flying from his head and high into the air, to land in a horse trough.

Taking advantage of the confusion, Hiram Trask rammed his spurs into his horse's flanks and galloped away. Spooked, Diana's mare and the other horse bolted after him. Eyes smarting from the blinding clouds of acrid gunsmoke, Matt and Andy were too busy dodging bullets and returning fire to give chase. Trask started to veer from the middle of the street toward a wide alley looming ahead, to one side.

It was then that Jesse Seaton, cursing under his breath because of his missed shot, decided to risk another from his hotel window and took aim at Hiram Trask's back. He held his breath and squeezed the trigger. This time he was rewarded to see his target slump in the saddle, then slide from it, loose-limbed.

His spine shattered, there was only a spark of life left in Hiram Trask's body as he hit the ground and rolled head over heels into the path of the two runaway horses, whose hoofs stomped his head and turned his brains to jelly.

Despite the chaos around him, Matt had caught a glimpse of a red flash, and now noted the plume of smoke drifting out from a second-storey hotel window. Unsure if the shot had been meant for him, he sent a precautionary round through the open window. Then his rearing horse gave a deep grunt and abruptly toppled heavily to the ground. Matt just barely managed to extract his boot from the stirrup and hurl himself away, avoiding having his leg trapped beneath the horse's dead weight.

Clutching his six-gun, he rolled toward the water

trough where his hat floated. Searching slugs sang through the air and chewed up the ground about him, hurling small showers of dirt and manure in wild abandon. Somehow Matt reached the safety of the trough and, knuckling his eyes with his free hand, squinted out at the street.

Stretched out low in the saddle Indian style, Andy Denham was tearing after the horse and travois with its swaying, lifeless body. Should it spill out on the street, the truth would be revealed to one and all and the game would be up. No shots screamed after him; evidently now that Hiram Trask was dead there were second thoughts about shooting a lawman.

But there were no such qualms about shooting a stranger. Matt hunkered down behind the trough and, disregarding the whining bullets thunking into the wood and water, reloaded as quickly as he could, dropping a few shells in his haste. Peering around the side of the trough, he saw Andy catch up with the runaway horse a short distance past the sheriff's office and rein it in. Thankfully, Lonis's body was still on the travois. The deputy would have to deal with getting the body inside, or else wait for Matt to reach him. Though at the moment Matt's thoughts were on how to make his way back to the alley where Diana had been dragged and find out what had happened to her.

A shot from a rooftop directly across the street punched another hole in Matt's badly riddled hat and splashed water over the side of the trough and down his back. Risking it, Matt raised up and fired two rapid shots. There was a dying scream, then a rifle toppled over the edge of the roof and was followed by a man's loose-limbed form. Both crashed loudly on the wooden boardwalk before the building.

A gun flashed and belched smoke from an alley beside the building, and Matt heard the waspish buzz of a bullet as it sped past his ear. Holding back the trigger, he fanned his six-gun, emptying it. As the hammer clicked empty, a man's figure emerged slowly from the darkness and, spurs jingling, stumbled out into the street. His chest leaked blood, and it was obvious he was dead on his feet. The pistol at his side discharged into the ground as he tried to raise his arm. Then he pitched forward and landed heavily, face-down, like a dropped sack of grain. His body shuddered in its death-throes then was still, frozen in an awkward, unnatural position of violent death.

A funereal quiet settled over the street. The sight of the deaths of two of their comrades obviously had a very sobering effect upon the remaining men, who were only simple cowpokes unused to the deadly art of gunplay. Then Andy Denham broke the silence, bellowing in the most authoritative tone he could muster.

'Aw right now, that's all she wrote. It's over and done with. Hiram Trask is dead, and Wes is going to jail – so there's nobody to fight and die for but yourselves, if you've a mind to prolong this unlawful fracas.' He took a deliberate pause to allow his words to sink in, then went on, 'I know who most of you are, but since I ain't seen your faces you won't be charged. Though you sure as hell should be. If you all know what's best, you'll get on outta here and drift while you can. Stay around and you'll end up dead or in jail. Now git to it!' There was a long moment of silence, then the men were heard withdrawing hastily and Andy inwardly sighed his great relief.

During Andy's speech, Matt had reloaded, and on hearing the men leave, carefully left his hiding place and made for the alley. There were signs where Diana had been dragged and then carried to the end of the alley, but there the footprints merged with a tangle of others and were lost. He felt she must be near about – but where?

The sounds of departing horses caught Matt's attention. He saw several men riding out the back way instead of going into the main street where Deputy Andy Denham could recognize them. Nobody would be so stupid as to be seen by the others carrying away a helpless young woman, and Diana sure wouldn't have gone willingly.

Reluctantly giving up the idea of any pursuit for the moment, Matt turned and headed back to join Andy Denham. Despite what had happened, they couldn't just abandon their plan. Rafe Lonis's lifeless body had to be put in a jail cell, in hopes the real murderer would still make another try to silence him. If anyone but Matt helped Andy do so, the deception would be uncovered and the killer would never be caught.

Besides, Matt needed help to search the strange town, and Andy Denham probably knew the most likely places frequented by Wes Trask. He was without a horse and needed to find Diana's mare, until the livery stable was open and he could buy another mount. One way or another the price would come from Wes Trask, whenever he caught up with the cowardly little bushwhacker.

CHAPTER
SEVENTEEN

Surprisingly his father's death was not the tragedy
Wes Trask had once imagined it would be. Sure,
there was the righteous desire to avenge the killing of
a blood-kin. Still, he was now free of the love/hate
relationship, and the frustrated feeling that nothing
he could ever do was quite right in the old man's eyes
– and there would be no more of him being belittled
in front of others, especially the hired hands. He was
now sole boss of not only the ranch but the town. He
had to act fast to still keep control of the town, and
that meant putting that upstart deputy six feet under
in Boot Hill. The same went for that shootist pal of
his.

The girl's muffled gasps and desperate struggles in
the hay distracted his thoughts and Wes scowled over
at the last stall in the livery stable, where Diana
Logan lay wrapped tightly from slender shoulders to
booted ankles in Chuck Rand's saddle rope. A folded
bandanna between her lips held a wadded cloth
inside her mouth, and her delicate nostrils flared

wildly with her laboured breathing.

'Might as well settle down, girly,' Chuck Rand taunted, eyeing her heaving breasts straining between the sunken rows imprisoning her arms and torso. 'You ain't a-goin' nowheres less'n I'm of a mind to turn you loose – which I ain't.' He grinned nastily then asked, not taking his dark lecherous eyes from Diana, 'When's the fun gonna start?'

'After I brace that deputy. The sheriff's a-bed, dying, so then there will be no more law in Willow Creek but me, which is like it should be.'

Rand stepped closer and prodded Diana's hip with the toe of his boot. 'Supposin' her man takes a hand?'

'He won't because we have his woman. Tomorrow I'll telegraph around, and in another day or two this town will start filling up with hard-cases.'

'Sutton wants his woman back, and he ain't gonna sit idle whilst you go to building up an army,' Rand said, and hiked Diana's rumpled skirt higher up her thigh with his toe. 'Ain't that right, sugar?' he jeered, then grinned widely as she stopped thrashing and glowered up at him, pure virulence in her large, glacial blue eyes. 'I surely do love a woman what hates,' he said, unintimidated. 'Makes it all the more enjoyable when you finally get around to using her.'

'Leave her be for now and listen,' Wes said impatiently. 'We're doing for Sutton tonight, as soon as I've dropped that deputy. Now here's how we'll do it.'

Since the gunplay was apparently done with for the

night, the saloons relit their lamps and opened for business. One of the customers at the Long Trail Saloon was Elijah Hobson, who had no pressing reason to make the long ride to his lonely ranch just to sit there and drink and brood alone. He had no want of company now, but having people around offered an occasional distraction from his dark thoughts. The gamblers and house girls knew to leave the burly, brooding man to his privacy at a far corner table.

The more Elijah Hobson drank and thought, the more he honestly didn't know if he ever cared to return to the plain and badly weathered ranch house, whose recent, violent memories far overshadowed the few happy ones he could recall. A simple, taciturn man, he was unused to saying the niceties that a woman longs to hear, and when he'd tried the words usually had sounded forced. Still, he had truly loved Ellen and thought she felt the same about him. Even the times she had seemed moody and distant he'd taken into consideration their hard life, and more recently, her concerns over having a child, which they'd both wanted.

Then a darker, more unsettling thought came to mind, and though he tried to dismiss it as liquor playing hell with his brain, the more it made sense. Neither he nor Ellen had any enemies, and if the prisoner was indeed innocent, what was the reason for her murder? Could it be that she loved somebody else, maybe even enough to have his child, and that person killed her rather than have the truth come out? No man likes to think of himself as a cuckold, but that reason sure offered up a damn good reason why Ellen was murdered.

Hobson slammed the side of a fist down, hammer-like, on the table top and loudly uttered a string of sulphurous oaths. Heads turned, startled, then quickly turned away, not wanting to incur his drunken wrath. He paid them no heed; he was already laying plans to watch the jail until he uncovered the killer. Evidently the prisoner had seen or heard something that would incriminate the man, and Hobson was going to be around when he either regained consciousness or else the killer made another try for him.

Bathed, shaved, and wearing a fresh set of town clothes, Jesse Seaton left his hotel room with his rifle under his arm to join Andy Denham and Matt Sutton at the jail. From his window he had seen the two take Rafe Lonis from the travois and into the sheriff's office. He had to know if the man's condition would allow him to recover, and if so, then he had to somehow see that did not happen. Again, he cursed his missed shot when that damn lasso came flying out of the alley and pulled Diana Logan from her saddle, startling both horses. Well, at least he'd managed to take care of Hiram Trask.

Seaton smiled at his accomplishment as he went down the stairs, then remembered to put on a sombre expression as he reached the lobby. He needn't have bothered, the mousy desk clerk was nowhere to be seen. The gunplay must have sent him scurrying off to safety, and he had yet to return.

Stepping out on the boardwalk, Seaton saw the carnage still remained. Sutton's dead horse was nearby, the two 'punchers lay across the street, and the once high and mighty Hiram Trask was littering the middle of the street with his brains spilt out for folks to step on. Somebody needed to clean up the mess before it drew flies, curs, and maybe even a buzzard or two. Seaton wanted the town he'd just inherited to be neat and clean, as he had big plans for turning it into a money-making metropolis, such as Abilene or Dodge City, and it wouldn't do for speculators from the East to arrive and find the streets littered with corpses.

Seaton walked a distance past the bodies before starting to cross over to the sheriff's office, but halted beside a wooden awning post as he saw Wes Trask come out from an alley ahead of him. Curious, Seaton remained there half hidden and watched him stalk purposefully toward the jail.

Having deposited Rafe Lonis's corpse in a middle cell in the cellblock, Andy Denham and Matt Sutton had returned to the front office and were discussing whether to bring the town doctor in for show.

'It means letting him in on the truth,' Matt said. 'Can you trust him not to talk?'

'Doc Hardin has been practising here for nigh on to twenty years, and everybody agrees he's an honest and dedicated man.'

'Then he oughta want to see justice done. You go fetch him and I'll mind the store. Don't take too long. I've still gotta find Diana.'

Before Andy could speak, Wes Trask's harsh voice came from out in the street. 'Hey, in the jail. I'm here for a face off with *Deputy* Denham. Come out and meet me in a fair, stand-up gunfight, or turn over your prisoner and leave town with your tail betwixt your legs.'

Andy and Matt exchanged surprised glances. 'Let me handle this,' Matt said coldly.

As though he had heard Matt, Wes Trask added, 'Stay out of this, Sutton, if you ever want to see your lady friend again. This is strictly a hometown affair.'

'He's right,' Andy said quietly. 'I've gotta face him some time. Besides, you're not gonna always be around to hold my hand.'

Matt considered, then nodded. 'All right, but let me give you some advice.'

'I'll take all I can get,' Andy said, and forced a smile.

Jesse Seaton could scarcely believe his good fortune. Here he was about to witness a shoot-out between the town deputy and Wes Trask, the last man needed to be removed to ensure his complete take over of the town. Should Trask kill Denham, then he, acting as a good, law-abiding citizen would be compelled to shoot the law-breaker dead. Supposing things went the other way, then Denham would have done his job for him, and Seaton would congratulate him and follow his original plan to help guard the jail against any irate citizens and use the opportunity to stealthily see that the prisoner never awakened from his coma. He tensed expectantly as the door to the sheriff's office opened and Deputy Andy Denham stepped out, straight and tall.

Wes Trask grinned eagerly and took a crouched gunman's stance as Andy Denham stepped off the boardwalk and strode toward him. He waited for the deputy to stop and make his play but he kept right on coming.

'Hold it, Denham,' Wes called, confused. 'That's far enough. Now make your fight.'

Andy Denham ignored him and wordlessly kept right on marching straight at him. Wes saw that the distance was quickly becoming too close. Any gunplay and both participants stood a good chance of being hit, even killed. That wasn't how it was supposed to be. He took a quick step backward and went for his guns.

That was Wes Trask's second mistake. Besides the moment of hesitation, he tried to draw both guns at once, something a real gunfighter never did, as it slowed his draw by seconds and in a gunfight every second counted.

Andy Denham had his Colt out before Trask's guns cleared their holsters. Seeing he was outdrawn, Wes again hesitated indecisively. 'Don't do it, Wes,' Andy said, a trace of reluctance in his tone. 'I don't want to kill you.'

Wes Trask caught that slight reluctance and reached his decision. The twin guns started to raise. It was his third and last mistake.

Before Andy Denham could pull the trigger, the strained silence was shattered by a rifle shot.

Six-guns blasting into the earth, face mirroring agony and disbelief, Wes Trask pitched forward and fell at the deputy's feet. For a moment Andy Denham stared down uncomprehendingly at the bloody hole in the centre of Wes Trask's back. Then he became aware of approaching footsteps and looked up to see Jesse Seaton crossing the street to him, smoking Winchester in hand.

'I was afraid you had buck fever, Andy,' Seaton said, feigning true concern. 'You know, he almost killed you.'

'I'd have seen he didn't,' Matt Sutton said from the open doorway, gun in hand. 'Dammit, we wanted him alive.' Holstering his pistol, he stalked forward.

'I'm sorry,' Seaton said lamely, and halted a few feet from Andy, who was kneeling over Wes Trask. 'I thought I was doing the right thing.'

Matt paid him no heed, knelt beside Wes Trask, who groaned and stirred feebly, and seized him by the shirt front, raising his face close to his own. 'Trask, where's Diana?' he demanded gruffly.

Trask's slowly glazing eyes blinked, focused, and for a moment intelligence glowed in them. Recognizing Matt, a taunting, malicious smile spread over his grimy face. Forming the words with difficulty, he said hoarsely, 'Livery ... stable ...' He started a laugh that quickly became a racking cough and died spewing blood.

Matt thrust the dead man away, letting him drop to the ground, staring up sightlessly, and turned to Andy. 'Where do I find the livery stable?'

*

Dishevelled blonde hair glimmering in the light of a full moon, Diana Logan stood writhing against a thick wooden post in the middle of the livery stable corral while Chuck Rand finished securing her already well-roped body in place with a separate lariat. She winced and uttered a muffled cry of anguish into her gag as he jerked the last loop sinkingly taut, then knotted the ends and stepped back to survey his work.

'That snubbing post is used for breaking and training broncs,' he informed her. 'And that's just what I'm aimin' to do to you, soon as all the nasty shootin's over.' He flashed a mocking grin, then turned and ambled toward the livery stable, leaving Diana to strain helplessly at her ropes and crane her neck to stare nervously after him.

Elijah Hobson took up a position that enabled him to watch the back door and length of the side of the sheriff's office, then settled down in a shadowy doorway with his whiskey bottle for what could be a very long wait. He had heard but not seen the shooting of Wes Trask and was indifferent about the end of Trask rule in Willow Creek. The Trasks had too much land, and even hogged in to claim well over half of the open range. Now other small ranchers like himself ought to be able to enlarge their own spreads, and maybe even encroach on Double Bar T land itself. The opportunities seemed endless.

At the present though, Hobson preferred to dwell on finding the man who murdered Ellen, and felt confident that he would do so tonight. The way things had been happening, the killer should take advantage of all the confusion and make his play. When he did, Hobson would be ready and waiting to extract his own brand of vengeance.

CHAPTER EIGHTEEN

Andy Denham paced impatiently about the large office. He felt sure that Wes Trask had taken a dying man's revenge and Matt Sutton was walking into another trap. He should be siding Matt instead of guarding a dead man, whose killer might not even strike tonight. Still, Matt had insisted they keep to their plan and had gone alone, even rejecting Jesse Seaton's offer of help.

As if trying to make up for being taken in by Wes Trask and leading them into the ambush on Main Street, Seaton had stayed as an unofficial deputy to help guard the jail. With no more Trasks to rile things up, Andy doubted a lynch mob would form. Also, with too many guards around, the real murderer might not try to act. Andy was tempted to let Seaton in on the trap, but that knowledge might make him want to stay and help even more. And though Andy didn't think so, there was the possibility that Seaton was the killer and he would be upsetting the plan.

To be rid of Seaton for a time, Andy had sent him

to fetch Doc Hardin, as he and Matt had discussed. Besides, he wanted to learn how Sheriff Crandall was faring. Perhaps by the time Seaton returned, Matt and Diana would already be there, and Seaton could be diverted while Doc Hardin found that he was examining a dead man.

It suddenly dawned on Andy that the murderer might make a try while he was alone, and he made a perfect target, moving back and forth in front of the windows on either side of the front door. He took a seat behind the sheriff's big, battered and scarred desk and turned the lamp low. Loosening his Colt in its holster, he sat waiting and wondering who would be the first to walk through the door – a friend or the killer?

Danger and Matt Sutton were old enemies and understood each other. He wasn't so simple as to believe that Wes Trask, knowing he was dying, would repent his ways and benevolently tell him where to find Diana. Matt didn't doubt that Diana was at the livery stable, but he did doubt that she was there alone.

Turning the corner of the last block on Main Street, Matt saw the huge building a hundred or so yards ahead, on the edge of town. The tall, wide double doors were shut, including the one in the hayloft. Staying warily to the shadows running the length of the feed and grain store, Matt stole toward the silent barn with its long corral.

On reaching the end of the lengthy building, Matt paused to survey the vast open area remaining that he would have to cross in the bright moonlight.

There was still no sign of life but that didn't mean a thing. A rifle or six-gun might open up just as soon as he was halfway across, and with no cover he would die in his tracks, then and there. He looked up at the sky and was heartened.

Scudding clouds were drifting toward the full moon. They weren't much but there were no other cloud banks that appeared headed toward the moon. Matt waited restlessly, gauging the distance. The clouds wouldn't hide the moon long, and he had to reach the side of the stable and the corral by the time they passed. Was it his imagination, or were the clouds actually racing across the dark sky? No matter. He had to try it, regardless.

Colt in hand, Matt held to the shadows, steeling himself for the long dash the instant the clouds reached the moon. Despite their fast movement, they seemed to take for ever. And then they blotted the moonlight, and Matt Sutton ran for all he was worth.

Even though his pounding steps and heavy breathing sounded loud to his ears, no shots sought him from the blackness ahead. As fast as they had come, the clouds passed. Matt was still six feet from the corral when he was bathed in moonlight. Quickly, he made a long leap and rolled across the ground. Again, there were no gunshots. He came to a stop against a corral post, then wincingly sat up rubbing his back, and peered cautiously between the rails. His gaze roamed over the corral and froze on a slender figure standing lashed to a snubbing post.

It was Diana, gagged and held in place by numerous ropes, her long blonde hair silver in the moonlight. Like a sheep staked out to draw a bear or puma, she stood there waiting to be rescued – and somewhere inside the stable was the hunter, waiting patiently to make his kill. Only Matt was determined not to let Wes Trask have a dead man's revenge.

He belly-crawled along the corral to the side of the stable, slithered under the railing, then stood and, back pressed against the building, made his way silently to the rear. Slumped in her ropes and facing away from the stable, Diana did not seem to be aware of his presence, which was just as well as she might accidently tip his play. Reaching the corner of the stable, Matt eased around to the back.

The rear doors stood open, as did the one up in the hayloft. Matt needed to know if the man or men were down in the runway or up in the loft. There was only one way to find out, he had to go inside the stable. He searched the sky for more clouds.

This time there were none. The area around the moon was clear, with no clouds in sight.

Matt edged around the corner to the yawning doorway and hesitated, listening. No sound came to him. He ducked hurriedly inside and flattened against a wall, six-gun ready. The broad, moonlit runway was empty, as were the stalls. Judging his man or men to be in the loft, Matt stole along the stalls, further into the silent building, while squinting up and trying to make out anyone beside the open doorway above.

Framed against the night sky, a moonlit form crouched with a rifle resting on top of a bale of hay. He appeared to be alone, and his attention was centred down in the corral area where Diana was bound to the snubbing post.

Matt caught himself just in time and narrowly avoided knocking an unlit lantern from a stall post. Taking it off its nail quietly, he crouched inside the stall, holstered his pistol, then pulled a match from a shirt pocket and, raising the glass chimney, lit the lamp. As it glowed brightly, he stepped out into the runway and hurled it up at the man in the loft.

Glass shattering on impact, the lantern showered its fiery contents over Chuck Rand and the bale of hay. Yelling curses, he forgot the rifle and leaped up, swatting at his shirt and trying to kick the burning bundle of hay out the doorway. He made a clear target, and when he yanked out his six-gun, a hail of bullets smashed into his chest and drove him backwards on his heels against the tottering bale. Pistol hurling up dust, splinters, and bits of hay, he collapsed on top of the swaying, smoking and blazing straw. His added weight flipped the bale out through the open doorway, and both slammed to the rough earth below. Rand's dying, spasming body was pinned beneath the fiery bundle, and his muffled shrieks ended abruptly when the intense heat set off the bullets in his gunbelt.

Eyes huge with terror and confusion, Diana cringed rigidly against the post and turned her head wildly from side to side, attempting to see the happenings behind her. It sounded like a long string of large fire-crackers was exploding but she quickly realized they were gunshots. By craning her neck near the breaking point, she caught a partial glimpse of a flaming mound of straw. After the racketing gunshots finally stopped, there was only the soft crackling of blazing hay.

Then came a new distress.

Besides straw, the air was tainted with burning cloth and leather, and a far worse stench that caused Diana to shudder and her stomach to churn violently at the realization it was human flesh. Her fear intensified as she wondered who the victim was: Matt, her captor, or someone else? The desperation to know increased her nausea, which she fought back with difficulty. To vomit while her mouth was filled with a cloth and gagged securely meant she could only expel it through her nostrils, which could easily become clogged and she would choke to death on her own bile.

Matt was forced to wait until he was certain that all of the wildly discharging rounds in Rand's shellbelt had been expended before rushing from the stable and past the smouldering, heaping mess to Diana. Relief replacing nausea, she nuzzled against him and murmured into her gag while he held her tenderly, thankful that she had not been hit by a stray bullet. Then he stepped back and began the laborious task of freeing her from the entwining ropes.

CHAPTER NINETEEN

Jesse Seaton had a lot on his mind as he hurried back to the sheriff's office. Doc Hardin had said he would be along within the hour, as that was all he reckoned Sheriff Crandall had to live. That was fine with Seaton, as he wanted to install his own man as sheriff. Andy Denham was out, since he had started taking his job too seriously and, having tasted power, would probably insist on being his own man. All the shooting from the direction of the livery stable had stopped, which meant Matt Sutton was either dead, or had rescued his lady fair. Sutton was also someone who wouldn't take orders subserviently, so tomorrow Jesse Seaton would compile a list of likely candidates, both in Willow Creek and elsewhere.

At the moment, he had to reach the jail before Sutton possibly returned and kill Rafe Lonis once and for all. It also meant doing for Andy Denham. That was too bad, as he rather liked him, but, like promises, friendships were made to be broken. Nothing was going to hinder his ambition. Tomorrow morning the sheep would finally come out of their homes and find they had a new town boss.

Deep in conversation, Matt Sutton and Diana Logan left the livery stable and made their way along the quiet streets toward the sheriff's office.

'I'm sure I saw a gunshot from the second floor of that hotel Seaton went in,' Matt said. 'But later, when the Trask hands were high-tailing it by back alleys so Andy wouldn't see their faces, no one came out of the hotel.'

'Perhaps the man left earlier, before you reached the alley.' Matt shrugged, and they walked on a few feet, then Diana remembered something and stopped, turning to him. 'Matt, when I was pulled off my horse there was a gunshot behind us, and we had just passed the hotel. The horses shied and the bullet struck a travois pole.'

'I remember a shot that came an instant before everybody opened up. I took it to be a signal.' He was thoughtful for a few seconds, then asked, 'I saw the bullet mark on one of the poles while Andy and I were moving Lonis's body into the jail. You're sure it happened right before things went bad, rather than later?'

'I'm positive,' Diana said. 'But I didn't see who fired the shot.'

'Whoever did was a pretty poor shot, unless he meant to hit Lonis and the spooked horse ruined his aim.' He was thoughtful again, then added, 'Neither Andy nor I shot Hiram Trask. We thought he was hit by a stray bullet from one of his men.' He continued on, 'Seaton shot Wes Trask when there was no reason. Andy had Wes cold, and I was backing him from the doorway.'

'Suppose Jesse Seaton is the man we've been looking for, why would he also kill the Trasks?'

'Hiram Trask ran this town; with both him and his son out of the way Seaton could take over.'

'It's all speculation,' Diana said, acting the voice of reason. 'We have no proof of his intentions.'

'We will if he makes a try for Lonis,' Matt said. 'And Andy's there alone with him.' He took Diana's arm and they hurried on.

Jesse Seaton entered the sheriff's office and found Andy Denham at the stove making coffee. As he told about Doc Hardin, Seaton moved casually to a heavy, well-worn sheepskin coat on a wall peg and took it down. 'Soon old C.J. won't have any more use for this.' He held it up before him. 'Many's the time I've seen him making his rounds in this coat.' He eased one of his six-guns from its holster. 'He used to say it was good protection from a man's fists, and would even slow down a bullet.' Aiming at Andy's back, he bunched the thick coat over the pistol's muzzle and squeezed the trigger.

Smiling in remembrance, Andy turned with the coffee can in his hand and started to speak. The muffled shot intended for the middle of his back struck him in the right side of his chest. Its brutal impact hurled him backwards, coffee grounds flying abbut wildly. He slammed against the stove, over-turning the coffee pot which spread its hissing, rapidly evaporating contents over the hot metal top, and sprawled to the floor on his side. Slowly, his body sagged over and he lay face-down, motionless.

Clutching the powder-burnt coat, Seaton shoved his smoking six-gun back into its holster and rushed to the cellblock door, only to find it locked. He whirled, lunged to the desk, and began yanking drawers open, searching. The key ring was in a side drawer.

Returning to the door, Seaton fitted the jingling keys hastily into the lock until he found the right one. He shoved the door wide open and strode into the corridor with the coat and key ring. He'd forgotten the lamp and was tempted to go back for it but a trisected shaft of moonlight revealed a still form on a bunk in a middle cell. Seaton went to the cell door and again fumbled with the various keys.

Finally a key clicked in the lock and Seaton jerked the door open, smashing himself painfully in the shoulder in his eagerness. Cursing his clumsiness, he stepped inside the cell and drew his Colt as he approached the blanketed figure. The barred window cast distorting shadows across the face, but Seaton knew it was Rafe Lonis. Muffling the sounds with the heavy coat, he fired two quick shots straight down into Lonis's face, turning it to red ruin.

Stepping back and discarding the coat, Jesse Seaton returned his pistol to its holster and grinned his relief. It had taken patience and a bit of doing but he had finally taken care of the last loose end and there was now nothing to stop him from assuming leadership of the town. He walked from the cell and was about to lock the door after him when the office door flew open and Sutton and his woman burst in.

Caught completely by surprise, Seaton was rooted in place in the middle of the corridor, staring at the two dumbfounded. The woman gasped and went to Andy Denham while Sutton pulled his Colt and came toward the open cellblock door.

'Hold it, Seaton,' Matt called sternly.

'Wait a minute,' Jesse Seaton called, his voice feigning innocence. 'I came in and found Andy dead and the cellblock door open. I went to see about the prisoner and also found him dead, shot in the face. I just came out of the cell when you two arrived.'

'Andy is still alive,' Diana called to Matt.

Her words brought a realization that his big dreams had ended in failure and Seaton dropped all pretence and ducked back into the cell, drawing both guns. The bars gave minimal protection and he knew he had to get out of the cellblock as fast as possible. Matt Sutton's voice came to him as though down a long tunnel, asking why he had murdered Mrs. Hobson, and Seaton saw no reason to hide the truth any longer.

In spite of the excessive amount of whiskey he had consumed, Elijah Hobson was alert. Earlier he'd come close to dozing off but the sounds of what he believed were faint gunshots had roused him from his lethargy. Since there had been no dying screams or anybody charging out the back door of the jail, he'd dismissed the sounds and remained slouched in the doorway across the alley. Now he heard shouting voices, and one that he readily recognized as belonging to Jesse Seaton.

Curious, Hobson dragged himself up and lumbered to the back of the jail, where he stood, eyes squeezed shut in an attempt to magnify his hearing, and listened to Jesse Seaton confess to murdering Ellen. A red rage boiled within him as he heard his doubts confirmed: the child was not his own.

Twin guns blazing and forcing Matt Sutton back from the cellblock door, Seaton broke from the cell and pounded along the corridor to the back door. Shoving a gun in its holster, he pulled back the bolt, jerked the door open and, again drawing his second Colt, barged outside where he abruptly found himself face-to-face with murderously scowling Elijah Hobson. Before he could recover from the shock, Hobson's huge hands closed about his neck and began throttling the life from him.

Gasping and struggling desperately as he felt himself lifted off the ground, Seaton rammed the muzzles of both Colts deep into Hobson's belly and fired their remaining rounds.

Hobson growled his agony as his body bucked and swayed with the force of the searing lead that tore through his guts but refused to loosen his death-grip. Feeling his strength ebbing with the warm rush of his life's blood down the front of his body, Hobson put his last ounce of strength into a savage wrench that almost turned Seaton's head completely around on his shoulders and snapped his neck with a loud, sickening pop.

In unison the two foes slumped to the ground in a bloody, grotesque tangle. And that was how Matt Sutton found them minutes later. Seeing that justice had been served, he leathered his Colt and walked back inside the jail.

In the front office, Matt saw Doc Hardin, a thin, elderly man in a black town suit, tending Andy Denham while Diana looked on. 'How is he?' Matt asked quietly.

'The bleeding's stopped,' the doctor replied, not looking up from his work. 'We'll have to get him to my office for me to remove the bullet.' He looked up and smiled. 'But he'll pull through just fine.'

'That's more than can be said for Seaton and Elijah Hobson,' Matt said before Hardin or Diana could question him.

A week later Matt and Diana looked in early one morning on Andy Denham, who had been elevated to permanent sheriff though he was still bed-ridden for the present, and made their good-byes. Then they resumed their long journey to California.

It was mid-summer when Matt Sutton and Diana Logan drew in their mounts on the bank of the Colorado River and stared across at California. They sat silently reflecting on their seemingly endless trek. At times, it sure seemed they would never reach their destination. But there it was straight ahead. California and a new life were waiting on the other side.

'Ready?' Matt asked quietly.

Diana nodded and smiled radiantly. They pushed their horses forward and, without a backwards glance, crossed the river and left the past behind.